Sinful Union

AN ARRANGED MARRIAGE MAFIA ROMANCE

THE ROMANO MAFIA
BOOK TWO

IVY DAVIS

Copyright 2023 by Ivy Davis - All rights reserved.

In no way is it legal to reproduce, duplicate, or transmit any part of this document in either electronic means or in printed format. Recording of this publication is strictly prohibited and any storage of this document is not allowed unless with written permission from the publisher.

All rights reserved.

Respective authors own all copyrights not held by the publisher.

ISBN: 9798854279284

CHAPTER 1
Natalya

My wedding day is crystal clear in my mind. It always will be. Luca and I said our "I dos" after the challenges we faced to get here. Standing before him on the raised platform before an audience of people, most of whom I don't even know—men who work for Luca or my father and their wives or girlfriends. I was sheltered from this mafia world growing up, but now that I'm on display on my wedding day, everyone has been called upon to attend. There's no more hiding. I know the truth.

I know my dad, Alek Antonov, is the biggest mafia boss in New York City. Luca is right behind him in terms of power. This marriage between Luca and me will help bridge the divide between the Russians and the Italians. I hope so, anyway. My dad isn't keen on me marrying Luca. In fact, he wants nothing to do with me now that I've gone down this path. It hurts me to my core, but if I choose my family, I'll lose Luca, and I'm not willing to do that.

Dad only agreed to my marriage with Luca because he caught Luca and me in a compromising situation. So, to protect my honor, he allowed me to marry him. But at the cost of losing him, it doesn't make my decision easy.

Looking into Luca's eyes, though, as we exchange our vows and rings, I know I made the right decision. My family is my past. Luca is my future.

The love I can see in Luca's eyes warms my heart. I know he loves me—he's told me. And I love him. Everything is perfect. Nothing can change this moment. This beautiful, perfect moment.

Luca and I share our first dance in the reception ballroom of the hotel our wedding is being held in. The room is decorated in warm tones—browns and pinks, like a fantasy fall day. It also smells like vanilla, which wafts over me as I dance with my new husband.

"Wife," Luca says, so only I can hear. Our guests watch as we dance together.

"Husband."

His lips twitch in a way that makes a shiver pass over me. "We're finally married."

"I know. I never thought it would happen."

"I did."

"Confident, are we?"

He pulls me closer, his hand resting on my low back, keeping me in his embrace. "Yes."

The kiss he gives me is perfect—light and airy. Appropriate for a room full of guests, including my parents. My eyes land on my dad over Luca's shoulder to see him scowling at us.

I sigh. "He's not happy."

"Then ignore him." Luca turns me around, so I'm facing away from my dad. "I'm your husband. You're mine now. You don't need to concern yourself with your family."

"He's still my dad, Luca. He always will be. And now that you're married to me, you'll probably have to do business with him. So, I ask that you two get along."

"Hey, I'm more than capable of getting along with your dad. I'm the one who reached out to him to form an alliance, to begin with. He's the one who hates me. Maybe you need to ask him to play nice."

"I would, but he's icing me out. Punishment for choosing you."

"That's not very nice, is it." He kisses me behind my ear.

My breath comes out faster, and my body tingles. "No, it's not."

"You have me now, Nat. Just focus on us. No one else. Just us."

"Ok." And I want to. With all my being, I want to focus on Luca, but my heart is still torn. My family is my family. Even though my mom, Katia, has made it clear she'll always be there for me, my dad *is* punishing me for my choice. It's hard to have your heart pulled in two directions—between the man who raised me and the man who's now my husband.

The rest of the reception goes by fast in my haze of excitement. Luca and I dance some more, laugh, eat, kiss. I'm so happy with him that it almost hurts.

But I'm even more excited about what will happen tonight. Our wedding night.

Even though Luca has touched me all over, we haven't actually had sex yet. He wanted us to wait for our wedding night. I know he's not a virgin, but I am. He wanted me to be pure in every sense of the word for tonight. Now, I'll get to be with him, and my body can barely take the anticipation.

When it's time for Luca and me to leave the party, I must resist the urge to run right out of there and up to our hotel room. After tonight, we're going to Italy for our honeymoon. I'll be entirely in Luca's domain, and I'm ok with that.

Mom comes over to hug me goodbye since Luca and I will be leaving for our trip first thing tomorrow morning. "I love you, honey."

"Thanks, Mom." I squeeze her tightly back, needing to hold onto her for a moment longer. Even though I'm excited to spend my life with Luca, it's still intimidating. It'll be strange not to see my mom every day. "I love you, too."

She pulls back. "Have a safe trip. You know I'll be here when you return if you ever need me."

"I know."

Dad stands off to the side, not quite looking at me but facing my direction.

"Dad?" I say. "Can I get a goodbye, at least?"

His icy coolness cracks for a moment when he pulls me into a quick hug. It means everything to me. But before I can relax into it, he pulls away. "Be careful, Natalya."

"I will be."

His eyes flit to Luca behind me. "With him. Always be careful."

"He's your son-in-law now."

"I know. And that's not something I would've chosen for either of us."

"Why can't you just accept I'm growing up?"

He stares at me for a moment. "That's not the part I have a hard time accepting. It's who you're 'growing up' with." He lowers his voice. "Luca is dangerous."

"And you're not?" I know my dad has done bad things. You don't become a mafia boss without that.

He blinks. "Just listen to what I'm saying."

"I am, Dad. And I don't agree. Luca has never hurt me, and he never will. Now, I love you. And I hope someday you can accept my marriage." I look at Luca over my shoulder before turning back to Dad. "I've got to go."

Dad doesn't say anything more as I grab Luca's hand and walk out of the ballroom, entering my new life with him.

Our hotel suite is the definition of luxury. King-sized bed, soft drapes over the windows, warm lighting. It's perfect to spend the night with Luca. It's perfect to have my first time.

Luca carries me over the threshold, and the moment he sets me down, we're on each other before either of us gets a chance to breathe. His lips are intense on mine as he walks me backward to the bed. His hands on my waist are both a comfort and a thrill ride, knowing he could just slip them farther down and he'll have reached my most intimate area.

Our lips don't part even as Luca lowers me on the bed. We've had weeks of pining for each other, weeks of seduction, weeks of foreplay. Now, it's time to have it all.

"I need to get this off you," Luca growls as he grips the skirt of my dress.

"Then get it off me."

His eyes darken. "Fuck, you're perfect." He wraps his arms around me as he consumes my lips with his again. My hands grapple with his suit jacket, pushing it off him. I need to feel him. I need to feel all of him.

Even though Luca has seen all of me, I've never seen all of him. He's never asked me to touch him intimately, and I was too intimidated to ask. But now, that's all about to change.

Luca has me sit up as he undoes the buttons at the back of my dress. His fingers skim down my back, sending goosebumps over me. The best kind. He trails kisses down my back, following the path of his fingers. He doesn't go lower than my waist, which makes me ache even more.

Luca pushes my dress down until I'm in nothing but my bra and underwear. "Fuck," he murmurs before he grabs me around my waist and pins me onto the bed. I love the weight of him on top of me—so reassuring but also thrilling.

"Luca," I almost whine as I tug at his shirt. "Please."

He smirks as he sits back and takes his shirt off, letting me see his muscular chest. I run my hand over his defined stomach. He looks like he wants to eat me whole, and I would gladly let him.

Luca grabs my hand and kisses my wrist. That simple kiss sends a wave of heat throughout my entire body. He quickly gets rid of my bra as he gives my breasts attention. My legs rub together, trying to get some friction from my growing arousal. I've never felt this turned on before, never this alive, never this frantic.

I gasp when Luca rips my panties down. He's touched me between my legs before, even kissed me down there, but I don't think I'll ever get used to it. His touch will always make me feel unhinged and wild.

Luca kisses down my body until he's hovering over the area between my legs. So close to my sensitive nub.

"Luca, please," I repeat, gripping the sheets. "Please."

He gives me a look of pure darkness before lowering his lips to my bundle of nerves. I immediately cry out as intense pleasure fills my body.

Luca is like a demon, the way he kisses me down there. He leaves no part of me un-kissed, un-licked, un-touched. My body writhes against the mattress as he pleasures me with his mouth, sending me closer and closer to the edge. I can't take it anymore.

I grip the back of his head, pulling him down closer. The friction of his tongue on my nub is too much.

"Luca," I gasp out, my hips jerking up. "Luca."

He is relentless in his pleasure of my body. His tongue is a work of art, the way it commands mastery over me.

With one more touch to my nub, I fall over the edge.

I cry out as I come, holding his head still. Luca doesn't seem to mind. He continues to kiss my bundle of nerves, folds, everything.

It's only when my body calms down that Luca pulls back. He looks incredibly satisfied with himself, and I honestly don't blame him.

I watch as Luca takes his pants and underwear off, letting me look at his erection for the very first time. He's beautiful. His body is something else. But it's not his body I love—it's his presence, the way he makes me feel special. It's him.

Luca opens my legs wider and settles between them. I can feel his length so close to my opening. "Are you ready for me, baby?"

"Yes." My hands grip his shoulders, pulling him in closer to me. I need to feel him completely against me, nothing between us. Nothing else will do.

Luca presses his erection against my opening as he kisses me. This is it. He gently thrusts his hips forward before entering me completely.

It hurts just the tiniest bit—like a dull ache that feels a combination of good and bad. But the pleasure of having him inside me overrides any pain.

Luca settles inside me, allowing my body to get used to his being inside me. He kisses me deeply like he's trying to kiss my pain away. God, I love him.

Once I feel ready, I pull back from our kiss. "Luca, you can move."

He smiles darkly as he grips my thighs and begins to really show me what having sex can be like.

Every thrust of his body into mine sends a ripple of pleasure through me. Our chests are touching. Not even a sliver of space is between us. The way Luca holds me so confidently, so warmly makes my heart soar. How can Luca be a danger to me when he treats me this way?

True, Luca and I have done some dark things. I've seen him kill a man. I killed a man for him.

But despite this, I trust him fully. I'm not scared of him at all.

"Nat," he growls as he increases his pace, thrusting into me more firmly. I wrap my legs around his waist. Our breath mingles, becoming one as we finally have this moment together.

I can feel the stirring of another orgasm inside me. My body is warmed up and ready.

"Fuck, baby," he murmurs, grinding his hips against mine. "You feel so good around me."

"Luca." My fingers claw at his back. I don't even care if I draw blood. In fact, Luca would probably like that.

"Are you close?"

"Yes," I gasp.

"Then come for me, baby." He kisses me as he continues to thrust inside me. The combination of his words and what he's doing to my body is perfect.

Just perfect enough to make me come.

I cry out against his lips, his mouth muffling the sound. My legs tighten around his waist, my hands dig into his back, my entire body becomes fire.

Luca groans as he joins me, his release filling me up. Everything about him feels perfect.

He only pulls out of me when we're both spent. "Nat," he says in wonder as he lays beside me. "That was fucking amazing."

I smile so wide my cheeks hurt. "It was."

His fingers trail a pattern over my stomach. "Was it everything you hoped it would be?"

"Even better."

"Good. Because once your body is ready, we're going to fuck again and again. You're going to be so sore by the end of this honeymoon."

"Is that a promise or a threat?"

He waggles his eyebrows. "Can it be both?"

With Luca? Yes, it can be.

And it doesn't even bother me one bit. In fact, it just makes my body even more excited.

I'm so ready for our honeymoon.

CHAPTER 2

Luca

"Ready for Italy?" I ask Nat once we're seated on the airplane.

"More than ready."

We're in first-class seats with a divider, giving us privacy from the other passengers. Which means I get to touch Nat during the entire flight.

Last night was perfect. I knew waiting for our wedding night would make things sweeter. Knowing that I claimed not only Nat's body but also her soul when we married makes me the happiest man on this planet. She's completely mine and only mine.

Nat pulls out a book from her carry-on.

"What are you doing?" I ask.

"I was going to read. It's a long flight."

"I had another idea in mind." I grab the book from her and put it back in her bag. She looks at me curiously as I squeeze her bare knee. Thank god for skirts.

Realization dawns in Nat's eyes before she parts her legs just slightly. *Good girl.* I trail my fingers to her inner thigh but don't touch her pussy. I know she's already getting wet for me. I took Nat for the first time last night, and now, I need more.

"I can't stop thinking about you," I tell her as I draw circles into her inner thigh. Just knowing people are on the other side of the large white divider makes the moment more thrilling. "Your soft skin. Every freckle on your body. Every goosebump that comes up when I touch you just so." I skim my fingers down to her knee and back up. As if on cue, goosebumps rise on her skin. "Like that."

Nat's eyes darken as she leans back in her seat and opens her legs wider for me. "Luca, please don't mess with me."

"Are you aching for my touch?"

"Yes."

My favorite word.

I finally give her what she needs.

Her lips part when my fingers press against her pussy. I slide my fingers under her panties, touching her skin to skin. Nat places a hand over her mouth to keep herself from making a sound. The divider might protect us from view, but I'm sure if she gets too loud, others will hear. Honestly, I'm ok with that. Let the world know she's mine. But Nat is still modest in so many ways. It's cute.

It lets me know I can corrupt her even more.

I grind my palm against her nub, rubbing her faster. She loves friction. I know exactly how to get my girl off.

Nat's hips rotate up and down as she strives to get closer to my hand.

I grab her chin and pull her into a kiss as I continue pleasuring her with my fingers. Her moans are muffled by my kiss. Her skin feels warm. Her breath comes out in pants. She needs this.

I press down onto her nub, and it's just the thing to make her come.

Nat moans into my mouth, her body shuddering. I open my eyes to watch her because she's always a sight to behold when she comes. I can't miss it for the world.

Once she's done, I pull my hand back and straighten her underwear and skirt. "There. A perfect way to start our trip."

Her cheeks are flushed. She looks like she just got fucked. "I agree," she says, breathless.

WE ARRIVE in Sicily after hours of being on the plane. I continue to pleasure her throughout the trip with little breaks to give her body a chance to rest.

I'm ready to fuck her again and again on this honeymoon.

Nat looks entranced as we arrive at our hotel overlooking the Mediterranean Sea. Everything is sandy and warm and bright colors. It's like walking into a fairytale.

The moment we get into our room, I grab Nat and throw her onto the bed. We spend the next few hours exploring each other's bodies and fucking until we're too tired.

We're lying in each other's arms when I get a phone call. "I should check it," I tell her. Nat looks beyond fuckable as she pouts, naked in bed, half under a blanket.

I don't recognize the number. "Hello?"

"Ah, Luca, you answered," a man says.

"Who is this?"

"It's Romeo Greco."

A pit enters my stomach. "What do you want?"

"I heard you're in Sicily. I'd like to stop by and chat. I wanted to ask you why you killed my brother, Angelo."

Shit. I forgot all about Angelo's younger brother, Romeo. He prefers to spend his time in Italy than in the States, which means he's easy to ignore. I dealt with Angelo a couple of months ago. In fact, I killed him right before Nat's eyes. It was the first time she saw the real darkness within me.

And now, Angelo's brother, Romeo, has decided to make himself known.

I took precautions when finding our hotel, so I doubt Romeo knows where we are, but I'll have to keep an eye and ear out in case he shows himself.

"Romeo," I say after collecting myself, "I can't answer that question for you. Have a nice day." I promptly hang up.

"Who was it?" Nat asks.

I could tell her. She knows I killed Angelo. She'd be curious to learn more about Romeo, but I don't want to spoil our honeymoon. The news about Romeo looking for me could put a damper on things, and I'm not going to ruin my week of non-stop fucking my wife for anything.

"No one," I respond.

"You said Romeo. Who's Romeo?"

I lean down and kiss her. "No one you need to think about. Just some old friend. He asked to meet up, but we're on our honeymoon. No one's taking me away from you." Wrapping my arms around her, I roll her onto her back. "Now, ready to go again?"

Nat looks at me for a moment before nodding. "Ready."

She's observant. But she also just wants to be in this moment with me and won't risk it by asking too many questions.

I only feel the slightest guilt for lying to her.

CHAPTER 3
Natalya

Luca and I go out for dinner at a restaurant overlooking the sea. My heart fills with romance from the warm tones of the restaurant, the candlelight, and how Luca looks so handsome in his suit. I feel like the picture of excellence in a black dress that showcases my shoulders.

"To our honeymoon," Luca says, clinking his wine glass with mine.

"I still can't believe this is happening. I never got to travel growing up. My dad wanted me safe in our home, under his eye. But look at me. Married to an incredible man, honeymooning in Italy, feeling like an adult for the first time in my life."

"You never got the chance to be an adult before. I'm glad I'm able to give it to you."

"Do you know how stifling it is being treated like you're ten when you're twenty-one? It's exhausting."

Luca raises his glass. "To your birthday as well."

It's strange that I'm twenty-one now. I don't feel a day older. The only difference is I can legally drink alcohol. Nothing tastes sweeter—everything just tastes the same.

But I'm still so happy, being here with Luca.

Nothing can change that.

... until halfway into our dinner when three men arrive and sit at a table near ours. At first, I don't think anything about them. I'm too consumed with Luca.

It's Luca who notices them, and I see how he tenses just slightly. Luca hides it fast by smiling at me, but I see it. I always see Luca.

"Do you know them?" I ask, glancing over at the group of men. They look my way, making me uneasy. I turn back to Luca. "Do you?"

"No," Luca says after a beat.

"Are you sure? They keep looking over at us."

"Let's just enjoy our meal."

I take a bite of my pasta, but the flavor isn't as delicious as it was a moment before. Now, it's stained by the worry piercing my heart. "Luca, you're lying to me."

He sighs, setting down his fork. "I'm not. I honestly don't know who those men are. But ... I may know who they work for."

Before Luca can explain more, the three men stand up as if on cue and approach our table. One of them walks behind me, and I tense when I feel something cold pressing against my back.

"Come with us quietly," another one orders Luca. "Or we *will* hurt your girl."

Luca's eyes grow dark but not from arousal. From anger. "You're threatening my wife? Is Romeo stooping that low?"

"Just come with us. Both of you."

"Luca?" I ask. I realize now that it's a gun against my back. I have a *gun* against my back! I might pass out.

"Just hold my hand," he says, extending his hand to mine. I take it, and together, we stand up. The three men walk around us, guiding us out of the restaurant.

"You didn't pay your bill," the waiter calls, but Luca and the three men ignore him.

Once we're out of the restaurant, the men walk us to a sleek black car parked across the street. The only other people outside are the ones coming and going from the restaurant.

The leader of the three men opens the back car door. "Get in."

"I don't think so," Luca growls before spinning and punching the man with a gun trained on me. The man falls back, and Luca grabs the weapon, shooting him in the head two times. The silencer muffles the shots.

The second man goes for his gun, but Luca shoots him before he can. The last man runs for the driver's seat, but Luca shoots him next. Not in the head, though, the leg. The man groans as he falls to the ground.

Luca grabs him, drags him to our rental car, and tosses him into the backseat.

"Get in, Nat," he orders as he enters the car. I stand there in shock, everything happening in a matter of seconds. I look down at the two dead bodies on the road, knowing someone will see them soon.

"Shouldn't we hide the bodies?" I ask.

Luca growls. "Damn it." He gets out of the car and throws the bodies into the back seat. When the alive one cries out, Luca pistol whips him across the temple, knocking him out. "There. Now get in."

I do.

Luca drives us away from the restaurant and into a part of the city that we haven't explored yet.

"Have you been here a lot?" I ask. "You seem to know where you're going."

"I'm Italian, Nat. I've been to every part of Italy. Besides, I always have a place to store bodies in case I run into trouble."

"You came prepared."

"When it comes to your safety? Always."

I glance back at the two dead men and the knocked-out one. "You said you know who they work for."

"I think. Probably a man named Romeo Greco."

"Who?"

"Remember the man I killed, Angelo? Romeo is his brother."

"And he's coming after you?"

He squeezes the wheel tighter. "It looks like. Pretty ballsy of him to attack me in public. I guess he doesn't know that nothing will stop me from killing someone, even if other people are around."

I'm silent the rest of the way to wherever Luca is taking us. It's only when a thought hits me that I ask, "I remember you talking to a man named Romeo on the phone the other day. So, you know he knew you were here? And you didn't tell me this?"

"Baby, I didn't say anything because I didn't want it to ruin our honeymoon."

"I could have died, Luca! I'm pretty positive dying would have ruined our honeymoon."

"I know I didn't say anything, Nat, and I should have. But right now, I need to finish dealing with that one"—he nods at the back seat—"before he wakes up."

"Why didn't you just kill him right away."

"I need information, and hopefully, he'll give it."

Luca arrives at a run-down building in a part of Sicily that I don't think I'll ever want to visit again.

He's quiet as he drags the man from the backseat and brings him inside. I follow. The inside is even worse than the outside, with cobwebs everywhere and floorboards falling apart. Pieces of the ceiling are missing. Luca must have boughten it knowing no one would want to step foot into a place like this—so, no chance of anyone finding a body.

A dusty dining table takes up most of the room. Luca places the man on it before grabbing a box from a corner. Inside is a bunch of supplies, rope, duct tape, and knives. Luca really did come prepared.

"You have places like this all over?"

He nods as he ties the man to the table. "I'm always prepared for the worst. Since I knew we'd be here for a week, I knew trouble could happen."

"Trouble follows you everywhere, huh?"

He grins. "You know it."

But I'm not sure that's such a good thing.

My mind goes back to my dad at the wedding, warning me to be careful with Luca. I thought he was telling me that Luca would hurt me, and that's just not true. But now I realize my dad may have meant that danger follows Luca, and whoever is with him could be in danger, too.

I had a gun pressed to my back tonight. That's the first time that has ever happened, and it was terrifying. I never want it to happen again.

That's the price I paid to be with Luca. I'm in a dangerous world now.

Luca slaps the man across the face, waking him up. He jerks awake, struggling against the ties. "Who are you?" Luca asks.

"What? Where am I? What the fuck?"

"I'm only going to ask once more." Luca dangles a knife over the man's eye. "Who are you?"

"Matteo," he spits out.

"Great." Luca's smile is easy, almost like he's not torturing a man right now. "And who do you work for?"

Matteo grimaces.

"You know I'm going to torture you. I can make this fast or slow. Answer me."

Matteo finally sighs. "Romeo Greco."

"I figured. How did he find me?"

"He has eyes and ears everywhere. He's coming for you. Now, let me go. I won't kill you. I'll just walk away."

Luca looks at me briefly before turning his scary eyes back onto Matteo. "I don't believe you." Luca jams his knife straight into Matteo's chest, killing him instantly. I don't look away. I can't. Luca's darkness is now my darkness, too. What's mine is yours and all that. Marriage.

HE wipes the handle of the knife clean before turning to me. My eyes widen as he approaches me and grabs me around the waist, kissing me deeply. Torture is a turn-on for Luca. And the way Luca touches me is a turn-on for me.

I gasp when he presses me against the wall. "Luca, this place is disgusting."

He steps back and takes off his jacket, lying it on the floor. "There. Better?" He grabs my waist and lowers me onto his jacket. There's a frenzied energy about him that only happens after he's killed someone.

When he touches me between my legs, I'm surprised to realize that I'm wet. Maybe torture is a turn-on for me, too.

Spreading my legs wide, I let him pull my panties down. Luca slips his erection out and presses it against my entrance. We moan in unison as he enters me in one thrust. I immediately wrap my legs around his waist, pulling him in closer as he kisses me, his lips so rough they almost hurt.

I clutch at his back as he thrusts into me. My body has adjusted to him inside me in the many times we've had sex over the course of our honeymoon. Despite this, I don't think I'll ever quite get used to this feeling. It's all-consuming. It's like fire, lighting me up within.

"Luca," I gasp as he grinds his hips against mine. Our first time together was so loving and gentle. This time is rough and wild.

My eyes land on the dead body of Matteo as Luca takes my body. I don't feel bad for Matteo one bit. He tries to kill my husband and me. He can rot in hell.

My thought process startles me. I'm not a bad person … at least, I don't think I am. But it's undeniable that Luca's darkness has taken root within me. I mean, we're having sex near a dead body, the man Luca just killed, and it's like it's nothing to me. I was more concerned with the building being gross than the torture and killing.

Luca fucks me harder, and I let him. I'm too caught up in my lust even to care.

With every thrust of his hips, his erection hits that perfect spot within me. The spot that sends shivers down my body.

I reach up and nip at his neck as I come.

Luca growls deeply and gently bites my neck in return, sending my orgasm to new heights. Soon, he soon joins me, and together, we moan out each other's names.

He rests on top of me for a moment once we've both calmed down. "You're amazing." He pulls out of me and puts his length away before fixing my dress.

"What are we going to do now?" I ask.

"Now, we head back to New York. Italy's not safe with Romeo

looking for me. I … need the power your dad can provide. His protection in case Romeo comes looking for us in New York."

"My dad won't offer it."

"We'll just have to make him an offer."

That's a threat, I know. It makes me uneasy—Luca and my dad going up against each other. They've already tried to kill each other a few times. Now that I'm in danger, this will only make my dad angrier. I'm not looking forward to asking for his help.

Back to New York we go.

CHAPTER 4

Luca

Nat and I go to her parents' house the moment we land in New York. If Romeo knew I arrived in Italy, he could surely figure out I'm back in New York. He's on a quest for vengeance, and I don't want Nat caught in the crosshairs.

When Alek opens the door and sees us, he scowls. "I thought you two were still on your honeymoon."

"There's something urgent we need to discuss with you," I tell him.

"Dad," Nat cuts in. "Please let us in. It's serious."

Alek grumbles under his breath but lets us inside. "Stay right there," he says when I step into the foyer. "I don't want you going any farther than that."

"Dad, now's not the time to fight," Nat says. "We're back early because we're in danger."

Alek scoffs. "I said this would happen."

Katia walks up behind him, placing a hand on his shoulder. "What would happen?" She looks at Nat. "You're back early."

"They're in danger, apparently," Alek explains. "I said this would happen. This is why I didn't want you to marry him." He swings his cold gaze from Nat to me, then continues, "What have you gotten my daughter involved in?"

"There's a man, Romeo Greco, who's coming after me. I don't want Nat to get hurt, so I've come to you for help."

"You got yourself in this mess, I'm sure. Can't you figure it out yourself?"

"You're the most powerful man in New York," I say. "My marriage to Nat also symbolized an alliance with you. Let's work together to build an even more powerful empire that will control all of New York for decades to come. To do that, we need to work together. I need your protection to make sure Romeo doesn't come after Nat or me. You don't want your daughter to get hurt because you didn't offer your help, now, do you?"

A sneer breaks out on Alek's face. "You're using my daughter against me. Forcing me to work with you."

"Dad, come on," Nat says. "Just work together. Luca is your son-in-law. He's part of the family now. When will you start trusting him?"

"Only when he stops putting you in danger. Which I'm guessing will be never."

"Dad, please."

Alek continues to look at Nat intensely before he sighs. "I'll agree to let Luca work for me if it means protecting you. But"—he sets his eyes on me—"that doesn't make us partners. You are not another mafia boss when you're around me. If you want my help, you'll be one of my employees. Can you handle that?"

My gut instinct is to say no. I've worked hard to achieve my success. I won't rid myself of power just to get Alek to like me. But when my eyes land on Nat, I know I'll say yes. She's too important to me. I can't risk her getting hurt when I have the opportunity to keep her safe.

"I'm at your service," I say through tight lips.

Alek smirks like he's won the war. He hasn't. The moment Romeo is dealt with, I'll go back to being my own boss. "Fine. You'll start tomorrow. I'll make sure Natalya is kept safe. I'll keep an eye out for Romeo Greco. But you're responsible for what happens to him. Understood?"

I nod. "Understood."

And just like that, it feels like I sold my soul to the fucking devil.

THE NEXT MORNING, I arrive at Alek's lounge as directed. "Reporting for duty, sir," I say, which I can tell irritates him. Granted, I don't think it would matter what I said to Alek. He'll be irritated, nonetheless.

"I have an assignment for you," Alek says, ignoring my greeting as he slides a piece of paper over. "Go to this address and collect the money owed to me and then bring it back to me."

I stare at the paper for a moment. "This is grunt work. I don't do grunt work. I have my own men do shit like this for me."

Alek leans back in his seat. "Did you already forget last night? I told you I would treat you like an employee. And as my employee, I want you to do this for me. Or I won't offer you my protection."

"You'd take it away from Nat?"

Alek stands up suddenly and gets right in my face. "I'll always protect my daughter. But I think you need my protection, too, and I won't hesitate to take it away from you if you get on my fucking nerves. And right now, you're getting on my fucking nerves, so I'd be careful what you say next."

I inhale deeply and let my breath out slowly. I can't fight Alek. I need his help. "Fine. I'll do this for you." I grab the paper off the table. "Anything else?"

Alek is quiet for a moment before he says, "No. You're free to go."

I head to the address written down, which ends up being a Russian deli. Entering, the scent of warm meat fills my nose. A stocky man behind the counter is cutting up slices of meat. "What can I get for you today?" he asks.

I lean against the counter. "I'm here to pick up an order for Mr. Antonov."

The man's eyes widen. "Uh … I don't know you. Normally, Sergei comes and picks up Mr. Antonov's order."

"Well, think of me as Sergei, then. I'm Luca." I hold my hand out. After a beat, he shakes it.

"I'm Vlad."

"Nice to meet you, Vlad. Now, I need that order as soon as possible because, as I'm sure you know, Mr. Antonov is not a patient man."

He frowns. "In my experience, I've found Mr. Antonov to be a very patient and understanding man."

"My mistake. I was talking about myself. *I* am not a patient man. Now, get me the order." So I can leave this damn place. My pride is hurting enough as is.

Vlad's eyes widen before he hurries into a backroom and comes out with an envelope. "Here's the order."

"Thanks." I grab it. "Nice doing business with you." I saunter out of the store and back to Alek's lounge. When I arrive, he isn't there. Instead, a blond man is in his place. Dimitri, Alek's second in command.

I approach him. "Where's Alek?"

"He had to run, but I'm here to collect the money. Hand it over."

I do, but I make a big show of sighing. "He couldn't even be here himself to do this?"

Dimitri smiles tensely at me. "Nope. He could not." He counts the money. "Good. It's all here. He told me to tell you that he expects you here tomorrow to do more work."

"Lucky me," I mumble.

"What was that?"

I smile brightly. "Nothing. I'm off. Tell Alek I have my own business to attend to."

My smile fades the moment I turn away.

I FEEL INSTANTLY CALMER when I get home and see Nat's beautiful face. "How's my wife?" I ask her, wrapping her in my arms.

"Great. I had a calm day. No men trying to hurt me."

"That's good." I kiss the top of her head.

"How was your day?"

I groan as I sit down on the couch. "Your dad has me doing grunt work."

Nat's lips twitch.

"Oh? You think that's funny?"

"Mmm-hmm," she says, nodding. "It's cute seeing you do what you have to do to help keep me safe. I appreciate it." She cups my cheek. "I love you."

"I love you, too. But I'm not happy about this. I'm a boss in my own right. I shouldn't have to do grunt work just because your dad is trying to put me in my place."

"It's the only way he'll offer his protection."

"I know. But it's humiliating. I'm a prideful man, you know?"

"Oh, trust me, I know."

I gaze into her eyes, so much like the color of the clearest ocean. "I have an idea that would cheer me up."

"Mmm. Let me guess. Does it involve you and me?"

I'm already bending down closer to her. "You know it does." Our lips touch.

It doesn't take us long to go upstairs and enjoy the rest of the evening, lost in each other's arms.

CHAPTER 5
Natalya

My heart is beating fast as I knock on my parents' door. Knowing that the house I grew up in isn't my home anymore is strange. I've only been living in Luca's home—now mine, too—for the past couple of days now, and while it's been amazing to live with him and have the freedom I've always craved, there's still an ache in my heart, knowing there's tension between my dad and me.

It's my dad who answers the door. I left Luca at home so I could talk to my dad in peace, "Natalya," he says icily. My dad isn't the warmest person, but he'd always treat me with care. It hurts that he's using the voice he uses for people who aren't close to him.

"Dad. Can I come in?"

He nods once, sharply, like we're conducting a business meeting.

"Did you need something?" he asks, turning away from me.

"Yes, actually." I plant my feet in the foyer. "You're giving Luca grunt work. He's not happy about it."

"It's the price he needs to pay to win my trust."

"Will you actually give him your trust if he does what you want?"

He doesn't reply.

"I didn't think so," I mutter.

"I don't see what the problem is. He's still a boss to his men. He can control them all he wants. He hasn't lost any power."

"But he hasn't gained any power either."

"Exactly. I don't want him to have any more power than he already does. He's most definitely not getting any of mine."

I fold my arms across my chest. "Are you even out looking for Romeo? He sent men after Luca and me in Italy. One of them … one of them put a gun against my back."

The iciness in his eyes shifts into a full-on inferno within a second. "You didn't tell me that before. I told you Luca was dangerous. That he'd get you into trouble. You could have been killed."

"But it was also Luca who saved me. Without him, I would have died."

"And without him, you'd never have been in that position in the first place. I never would have allowed it."

"That's because you never would have allowed me to do anything in my life!" I shout. "Sure, I'd be safe, but I'd be lonely. I'd be bored. Luca has awakened something inside me. He's given me life. Can't you see that?"

Dad jabs a finger at me. "And it's because of him your life could have been taken away in an instant. I'm not sure why this Romeo Greco is going after your husband, but I'm sure it's because Luca wronged him somehow. It's up to Luca to solve the issue. I have my men out there looking for him only for your safety. But Luca's on his own."

"Why can you just be happy for me?" I sob, surprised when tears spill from my eyes.

He stops. "Natalya." The pity in his voice breaks me.

Mom finally enters the foyer. I wonder how long she listened before coming to intercede. "Let's just all take a breath. Alek, I'm going to talk to Natalya alone. Leave us." Dad looks at her for a moment before walking away. Mom is the only person I've ever seen who can command Dad to do anything. It's inspiring, to be honest. And it's certainly not a skill I possess.

"Oh, honey." She wipes away my tears. "Come here." The moment her arms are around me, I feel safer.

"Why can't Dad forgive me for choosing Luca? I love Luca, Mom. He's my everything."

"I know you do. Your dad is struggling, for the record. He would never admit it, but I see the strain in him." She pulls back. "He loves you so much, and it's just hard for him to see you with someone he thinks is a danger to you."

"Luca isn't a danger to me."

"I believe that you believe that."

I step out of her arms. "Don't do that. Don't be condescending."

"I'm not trying to be. It's just … Luca is a wild man. He lives his life without worrying about others. I've seen other men like him, and it never ends well for them. I know you love him, and you have every right to. But your dad isn't wrong to say that Luca is putting you in danger. Whatever this conflict is with Romeo Greco, Luca needs to end it. I worry you'll end up as collateral damage in the process. I heard what you said to your dad. Men attacked you. You were held at gunpoint. How can we, as your parents, not be worried?"

I sigh, her words hitting me in my core. "No, it makes sense. I get that. I really do. But Luca is my husband now. Dad needs to learn to respect him. I don't know if I'll ever be happy knowing there's this tension between them."

"I understand. All I can say is, give it time. Let Luca prove himself to your dad. Then maybe, *maybe*, he will come around."

I laugh slightly. "Yeah, maybe."

Mom pulls me in for a quick squeeze. "I love you, honey. Just be safe for me."

"I'll try."

I TOOK the subway to my parents' house, so I have to walk back to the station. It's nearing sunset. Luca was at work when I left, so he doesn't even know I went to talk to my dad. I didn't want him to know what with them hating each other. I hoped my dad would listen and I could return home to Luca with good news. But that clearly didn't happen.

I know I shouldn't be out without a guard, but I've spent my life cooped up in a house, under constant supervision. I love to go for walks by myself now. I need it to feel like I can breathe.

I'm nearing the subway entrance when a black van pulls up beside me. Tension immediately fills my body. The side door opens, and a man steps out.

He has shoulder-length black hair and a scar right above his left eye. "Natalya Romano? I'm Romeo Greco. You should get in. We need to talk."

CHAPTER 6

Natalya

My first instinct is to run.

"I wouldn't think about running," he says before I can move. "I just want to talk. I'm not going to hurt you. I don't want you dead. I want you to deliver a message to your husband for me."

"I'll scream." Glancing around, I see people milling out, coming and going from the subway entrance.

"You could. But then you won't hear what I have to say. Get in the car, we'll talk, and I'll let you go. Safe and sound."

I know I shouldn't believe him. I should run away as fast as I can. But Romeo will surely catch me, and then who knows what he'll do to me? Right now, I need to play along and hope he's telling me the truth.

I nod once.

The smile that stretches across Romeo's face sends a shiver over me. "Great." He gets into the back seat, motioning for me to join him.

I do.

Once I'm inside, the car starts moving. "Hey, what are you doing?" I pound against the door.

Romeo settles in his seat. "Relax. My driver is just taking us away from here. But we'll drop you off near your home once we're done talking."

"You know where my home is?"

"Luca killed my brother. I've looked into him. Of course, I know where he lives."

"How do you know Luca killed your brother?"

"Because Angelo wanted Luca's job, and then he disappeared. I put two and two together."

"Right. Just tell me what you need to say."

Romeo leans in close. He smells like expensive cologne—musky and warm. "I want you to tell your husband I'm coming for him."

"Why not just attack us like you did before?"

He huffs. "Because Luca killed three of my men without any effort. He's a lot more dangerous than I gave him credit for. I guess that's why he's the boss. I can't just stage another attack. Something tells me he'll make it out alive. I need to be more strategic. I need him to be so angry that he's not thinking straight."

"And how are you going to accomplish that?"

"By talking to you right now. You're going to give Luca my message. I'll know if you don't. I'll know because I know Luca, and Luca will be furious when he finds out I took you. If he's not angry, I'll know you didn't tell him, and then when I take you again, I won't let you go."

I gulp. "I'll tell him," I whisper.

"Great." He leans back, giving me space to breathe. "Tell your husband I know where he lives. Tell him I won't hesitate to take you again. I want him full of rage."

"I'm not sure you want that. You're banking on Luca being so angry he won't hesitate to go after you. But an angry Luca isn't someone you want to mess with."

"I know what I want, Mrs. Romano. Give your husband the message." The car stops. "You may go."

I scramble out of the van, and the moment I step foot on the ground, it speeds off.

I'm down the street from Luca's house. Romeo wasn't kidding. He knows where Luca and I live. The thought makes me uneasy.

I hurry back home and wait for Luca to return from work.

My skips a beat when Luca returns home.

"How's my lovely wife?" he asks as I greet him in the foyer.

"Fine." He kisses my head, but I can't enjoy it. "Luca, listen. There's something I need to tell you."

He's in the middle of taking his jacket off and pauses. "What?"

"Romeo paid me a visit."

"What?" How he says it— so calm and controlled. It's honestly intimidating.

"I went for a walk, and he found me. He wanted me to deliver a message to you." I inhaled deeply. "He's coming for you. He wanted you to know he has the power to take me and won't hesitate to do it again. He wants you angry, Luca. He wants you to attack him so he can kill you, presumably. But I'm asking you not to get angry. I'm telling you we need to be smart about this."

Luca's hands clench around his jacket. "He confronted you in the street."

"No … he made me get into his car."

Luca's lips begin to sneer. "He thinks he can take you off the street and do whatever he wants to you?"

"He didn't touch me, Luca. He just talked to me. He wants you angry. Don't do this."

"Fuck!" He slams his fist into the wall, and I step back, startled. Luca sees my reaction and instantly calms down. "Nat. Are you ok? He didn't hurt you?" He pulls me into his arms.

"No, he didn't. He just scared me." I rest my head against his chest. His heart is beating fast. Luca is normally the picture of relaxed, even in the most stressful situations, so it scares me that he's nervous about this. "I'm ok, Luca."

"Your dad didn't keep to his promise. He was supposed to make sure you were safe."

"He can't have men everywhere. But I'll make sure that whenever I leave, I have someone with me. You. A guard. I'll be more careful from now on."

"Good. God, Nat. I could have lost you."

"But you didn't. Just promise me that you'll be smart about going after Romeo."

"I will be." He kisses me. "You're mine," he says against my lips. "You're mine, Nat. I won't let Romeo get his hands on you again."

"I know you won't."

As Luca kisses me harder, he presses me against the wall. I cling to him tightly, finding comfort in his touch, his body. He's so strong. It makes me feel stronger, too.

"God, I need you." He kisses down my neck. "I need you right now."

I gasp as he slides a hand between my legs. Before I met Luca, I would wear skirts on some days and pants on others. But since marrying him, I've only been wearing skirts.

He pushes my underwear aside and rubs my bundle of nerves. I'm already getting wet for him. His mastery over my body is almost intimidating, and I fall into it every time.

Luca rips my panties down, and I kick them away as I undo his pants and pull out his erection. He growls, his expression dark, as he kisses me harder.

I moan as he lifts me and wrap my legs around him, bringing his length to my entrance. Our eyes meet as we breathe heavily together before Luca enters me in one thrust. We moan, our voices mingling in beautiful harmony.

"Luca, Luca," I repeat like a mantra as he enters me again and again. The feeling of him inside me is so consuming. It's like I can feel Luca's love for me every time he touches me.

He grinds his hips against mine, making his erection press against that perfect pleasure spot inside me. My head rolls back, giving Luca the access he needs to pepper kisses along my neck. His strong hands are under my thighs, keeping up.

"Baby," he growls. "Fuck, I love you."

His words send me over the edge. I cry out his name as I come, which pushes Luca into a frenzy as he fucks me harder. He groans as he comes, too, his hand slapping against the wall.

"God," he says into my neck. "You're something else."

Luca helps me down and pulls my panties back up for me. He can be so considerate at times that I can't see how he can ever be a danger to me.

He gives me a sweet kiss before pulling back. "I fucking love you, Nat."

Whenever I hear him say this, it always sends me aflush with happiness. "I love you, too, Luca."

"I'm going to take a shower. Care to join me?"

I grab his hand. "Always."

We head upstairs. The only thing I feel is bliss. I'm not worried about Luca going after Romeo. I know he'll handle it like he always handles everything.

CHAPTER 7
Natalya

"What are you going to do about Romeo?" I ask as we lay in each other's arms. Luca's warm skin on my cheek is a comfort.

"I need to talk to my men about it. I can't rely on your father to provide the support I need. The issue is my men are spread fairly thin at the moment with a lot of different duties. But I'll make sure I have one keep an eye on you whenever you go somewhere without me."

"No privacy," I mutter.

He cups my face. "You know I need to."

"I know. It just sucks. With you, I've felt freedom for the first time in my life, and now, I don't even have that."

"It's just temporary until I can kill Romeo. He's slicker than his brother. He won't approach me like Angelo did, making it easy to kill him. I'll have to find him myself."

"Just be careful. And don't get angry. That's exactly what he wants."

He kisses the top of my head, the warmth from his lips putting me at ease. "I know. I had an idea for today. I want you to come with me to my meeting with my men. That way, you can get to know the people who'll help keep you safe in case you ever see one of them watching you or following you. Then you don't have to be scared."

"Ok. That would help. Thanks."

One hour later, I'm in the conference room of Luca's business—Romano Consulting. I know it's a legitimate business that he uses as a façade to keep cops from sniffing around at what he *really* does.

The room is filled with men in suits. I guess I imagined Luca's men looking rugged and dirty, like the underbelly of society, but no. They're just men in suits. I recognize some from our wedding day, which helps put me at ease. These are not men I need to be intimidated by. These men are here to help me.

I'm so nervous because my dad never included me in any of his business dealings. I'm still not fully used to this mafia world, despite my dad being the biggest mafia boss in the city.

Will Luca's men think I'm weak for needing their help? Will they objectify me? Or will they be kind and courteous?

"Gentlemen," Luca greets as we walk into the room. "Many of you know my wife, Natalya. She's here to observe our meeting today." Luca sits at the head of the table and has me sit beside him. His men don't grumble at the sight. They all give me a nod of acknowledgment, which makes me sit up straighter in my seat.

First, Luca goes through business topics that don't really concern me. Vague things about shipments. Money management—which I take to mean the money he collects from the businesses that owe him money. And basic security measures for Romano Consulting as well as other buildings he owns.

It's fascinating to hear Luca in action. How he speaks with so much conviction. How his men listen to him, enraptured. It's also a little funny knowing he needs to speak about the shadier sides of his business in a super vague way, presumably in case anyone is listening. It's bold of Luca to discuss things inside the conference room like this. I assumed most talks happened in dark alleys and booths at the back of a crowded club. But that's one thing I love about Luca—the way he's so bold in his life. It's how he won me over. It's clear it's how he wins others over, too.

Once he's finished discussing basic business, he finally turns his attention to me. "Gentlemen, I need you all to keep your eyes and ears out when it comes to Natalya. Romeo Greco has set his sights on her, and I don't want her hurt. I brought her with me today because I wanted her to get a good look at all of you so she knows you in case she sees any of you following her. Now, don't be creepy bastards when it comes to my wife. Keep your distance but stay close enough in case she needs your help. I'll be assigning a couple of you on rotational duty so someone always has an eye on her. Of course, that won't be needed when I'm with her. Understood?" Once they all nod in unison, Luca slaps the table. "Great. As you know, Natalya means everything to me. I don't want this weaselly little bastard to get his hands on her. Do your jobs and make me proud, gentlemen." Luca stands up, ending the meeting.

He motions for me to stand beside him, and as I do, I scan the men. I never thought I could feel this powerful in front of a group of people before. Sheltered as I was all my life, powerful men have always intimidated me. But with Luca, he has freed me of those fears. I can stand by his side and be just as powerful as him.

It's an intoxicating feeling.

In fact, it's an arousing feeling.

As they trickle out of the conference room, I turn to Luca and kiss him. He responds in kind, not even caring that we still have a small audience.

I gasp when he lifts me onto the table, pushing stacks of paper out of the way. It's thrilling.

Luca pulls back and glares at the men who haven't left yet. "Get out. Now."

They scramble out of the room, leaving just Luca and me behind.

"What's this for?" he asks, kissing me between words.

"You make me feel powerful. It made me want you."

"More than fine by me," he growls as he squeezes my waist, sending a flush over my body. My arousal grows by the second. I spread my legs, so Luca can fit nicely between them.

"Make me feel even more powerful," I say against his lips.

"Yes, ma'am," he teases before pushing a hand between my legs. "Wet for me, are you?"

"Always." I lean back on the table. "Please, Luca."

"I've created a monster." He pulls his erection out and pushes my panties aside, touching me where I desperately need to be touched.

"I think you're the monster," I tease back. "You're already hard for me."

"My sweet innocent, Natalya. When did you start speaking like that?"

"When you started corrupting me."

He smiles darkly. "Yes, I did."

I softly moan as he thrusts inside me. Luca's hand slap against the table as he moves in and out of me. I squeeze my legs around his waist, pulling him in closer.

I rest my entire back on the table, letting myself just feel in this moment. Feel the power coursing through me. I have a husband who's obsessed with me. Who loves me. And we're having sex on his conference table. Luca really has turned me into a monster. A wild, lustful one. I'd never known this kind of lust before I met him. He's ignited a fire inside me, and it refuses to burn out.

The sound of our bodies touching is almost dirty in the room's quietness. It turns me on even more.

Our breath comes out in pants as we get closer and closer to the edge. The look of lust and love in Luca's eyes is so powerful that it makes me come on the spot. I whisper his name, spurring Luca on. Soon, his own orgasm hits him.

He lowers onto his elbows and rests his head on my neck. I gently play with the hairs at the nape of his neck, soothing him.

"A monster," he murmurs into my ear before kissing a sensitive spot below my ear.

I just laugh.

CHAPTER 8

Luca

It's been a week since Nat had her encounter with Romeo. I listened to her and didn't react, even though everything inside me wanted to find Romeo and punch him until he died by my hands.

But I've been patient. I've waited.

Until tonight when I got a call from one of my guys stationed outside my house. "What is it?" I ask, keeping my voice down since Nat is asleep beside me.

"I just saw a man enter your house. I was going to stop him, but I figured you'd want the honors."

That's one thing my men know about me—I love punishing people. And I love me some good ole' violence.

"Thanks for letting me know. Just one?"

"Probably Romeo's guy thinking he can get you off guard. You didn't respond like he wanted you to. He's getting sloppy."

Hearing a creak on the stairs, I break into a grin. "I gotta go. I have a man to dispose of." I slip out of bed and grab my gun from the nightstand. Then I place a hand on Nat, waking her up. "We need to be quiet," I tell her. "Romeo sent a man here. He's inside the house. Just stay here. I'll deal with him."

She nods, her eyes open wide.

I keep my footsteps light as I walk to the side of the door. I don't open it. Let him come to me.

I motion for Nat to hide in the bathroom. She quietly runs to it, hiding behind the door. Now, I wait.

The man's footsteps get closer and closer until they reach the bedroom door. The doorknob turns, and the door opens an inch, revealing a face. He's got a round, chubby face that, under normal circumstances, would look inviting.

I don't give him another second.

I step forward and pistol-whip him in the head. He cries out, falling to the ground. I grind my knees into his back and keep him pressed to the ground, my gun against his head. "Did Romeo send you?"

He's quiet at first.

I dig my knees in harder. He groans. "Did Romeo send you?"

"Yes," he gasps out. "Can't. Breathe."

"Good."

Nat comes back into the room. "What are we going to do to him?"

"We're going to hurt him."

A wicked smile spreads across Nat's face. She really is my perfect match.

A FEW MINUTES LATER, we have him tied to a chair in our kitchen, a rag in his mouth, so no one can hear him scream.

"Do you want to do the honors?" I ask Nat, holding a knife out for her.

She grabs it without hesitation. "He came here to kill you, didn't he?"

"Probably. I found a gun in his pocket, so most likely. He probably would've killed you, too."

Nat walks up to the man and slices the knife across his cheek. He winces. "You don't get to come into our house and try and hurt us."

"Exactly." I have another knife in my hands, which I use to draw a small line across the side of his neck—not enough for him to bleed out, but enough for it to fucking hurt.

The man thrashes in his seat.

I take the rag out of his mouth. "What does Romeo know about me?"

He spits at me, but I just wipe it away. "If you're not going to answer, I'll have to cut you again." I lift the knife. "Your choice."

He looks between me and the knife before nodding. "Romeo knows you're a hot head. He expected you to attack him already. He was waiting for it. When you didn't, he sent me."

"Did you know he was sending you to your death?"

"No," he grumbles.

I guffaw. "You really thought you could beat me? Romeo really thinks that?"

"He does. He won't stop coming after you until you're dead." He looks at Nat. "Or her. He'll come back for her. He told me to tell her that he enjoyed their time together."

Nat slashes his arm deeply, making him scream.. "Romeo isn't going to have me. Luca will make sure of that."

"Of course, I will," I tell her. "Now,"—I look back at our prisoner—"normally, I would kill you. But I want you to deliver a message to Romeo for me." I lean into his ear. "Tell him if he fucks with my wife or me, I'll kill him slowly until he's begging for death. He won't see me coming until it's too late for him. He'll be looking over one shoulder for the rest of his life until I end it. Remember that word for word. I want Romeo to know."

I step back. Just for good measure, I draw a line with the knife down his face, from his forehead to his chin. A bleeding red welt is left behind. I didn't cut too deep. I didn't want to cause much damage. Much.

He slumps forward, mumbling pleas for me to stop.

"Give Romeo the message." I grab him, keeping him still tied to the chair, and toss him outside. He flops to the ground, struggling to get up with the chair still attached to him.

Then I slam my door shut. "Fucking bastard."

"What are we going to do, Luca?" Nat asks.

I kiss her head. "I'm going to go after him in a way he's not expecting. Once I'm done with him, he'll wish he were dead."

CHAPTER 9
Natalya

I get a call from my mom, asking if Luca and I want to come over for dinner. "Really? How does Dad feel about this?"

"He's not pleased, but he heard about Romeo sending a man to attack you, and he wanted to check in with you. Make sure you're ok."

"I am." I was in the middle of painting my toes when she called. I stroke the brush over my big toe, leaving behind an ocean-blue color. When Luca's at work, there's not much for me to do, especially with Romeo looking for me. It's safer to stay home. "Luca made sure I was safe. But yeah, I'd like to come over for dinner. I miss seeing you all the time."

"Me, too, honey. And as for your dad, he'll be fine. I told him I wanted this, and he backed down."

I chuckle. "You're the only person who can boss Dad around."

"It's because he values our marriage. Your dad and I have been through a lot together, but we've come out stronger. He wouldn't do anything to risk our relationship."

"He doesn't seem to extend the same courtesy to his daughter," I mutter before I can help myself.

Mom sighs. "He's just conflicted. He loves you and will always be there for you if you need him to. Just give him more time to come around. Your dad is a stubborn man. He's not easily swayed. But that's why I insisted we have dinner. It'll be good for all of us to sit down and enjoy a meal together. Maybe Luca and your dad can find some common ground."

"I hope so."

Because that's all I have—hope.

LUCA SEEMS ALMOST TOO giddy as we approach my parents' house. "You won't torment my dad, will you?" I ask him.

"Of course not. My mere presence will accomplish that."

I can't help but laugh. "Ok, fine. Just try not to get him riled up. Be polite. Be nice."

His eyes soften as he kisses my head. "Of course. For you, I'll do this."

My mom answers the door after we ring the bell. "Come on in." She takes our coats from us. "He's in the living room," she tells me as I look around the foyer.

I find my dad standing near the fireplace, staring intently into the fire. "Hi, Dad."

He looks at me, so that's something, at least. "Natalya." He starts to smile when his lips turn into a frown. I can feel Luca behind me. "Luca," he says curtly.

"Dad," he says, which I just know will upset my dad.

And he doesn't disappoint. Dad stands up straighter, glaring at Luca. "Don't call me that."

"But that's what you are." Luca settles his hands on my shoulders. "You're my dad now. We're in-laws."

"Dinner should be ready," Mom says, cutting through the tension. "Let's go eat." I'm pretty sure this distraction prevents Dad and Luca from getting into a fistfight.

"Be nice," I whisper to Luca, so only he can hear.

"All I did was call him 'dad.'"

"I know. But he thinks you're mocking him. Just be polite."

Luca and I settle into our seats, my mom and dad opposite us. My parents' housekeeper, Lizzie, brings out the food. The sound of clattering plates and clinking glasses helps fill the air, but the moment Lizzie leaves, a suffocating silence permeates the room.

Mom raises her glass. "To family." She nudges Dad. He grunts but raises his glass.

"To family," I say, nodding at Luca to raise his glass. We all take a sip and then start eating.

"I heard you had a visitor the other night," Dad says, cutting into his steak. Mom and I have faux meat dishes, while Luca and my dad have real meat on their plates. Despite the torture I've done with Luca, I still can't seem to eat animals. My mom has instilled compassion for them deep inside me since I was a kid. I justify hurting men with Luca because they've usually done bad things. They're not innocent animals.

"We did," I say before Luca can say something to piss my dad off even more. "But Luca handled him. I'm safe."

"Right." Dad looks between Luca and me intently as he sips his wine. "But the fact that Romeo managed to get a man inside your house, to begin with, is concerning."

Luca clears his throat. "I have one of my guys stationed outside our house at all times. He called me to let me know. There was no harm done. Unless you count the other guy." He whistles. "Nat and I sure did have fun hurting him."

It's like ice is poured over the entire dinner table.

Dad sets his glass down, glaring at Luca, and Mom looks shocked. I feel a blush cross my face.

"What do you mean you and *Natalya* had fun hurting him?" Dad asks.

Luca looks around the table, but he's not getting support from anyone. I didn't want my parents to know this, which says I know, deep down, that it's wrong what Luca and I have done. But it also feels strangely good to be in those dark moments with him.

"I just meant ..." Luca pauses. "I hurt the guy who tried attacking us. And Nat ... joined me."

Dammit Luca. I want to kick him.

"What do you mean by that?" Mom asks. "Natalya is kind-hearted. She'd never do anything to hurt someone, even if they deserved it. Right?" She looks straight at me.

In fact, both my parents are. It makes me feel like I'm twelve years old all over again.

"I didn't realize this was meant to be a secret," Luca says.

I shoot him a look before resigning myself to telling the truth. "Mom, Dad ... What Luca means is that ... sometimes when he's tortured a man ... I've been there. I've seen it with my own eyes. And ..." Here it goes. "I've helped him torture men in the past, including the one who came to attack us the other night."

Both my parents look at me like they don't even know me.

"How ..." Mom starts and stops. "How can you partake in that?"

A flash of anger goes through me. "Dad isn't a good man, and you stand by and let it happen."

"But I don't participate in it. I'm just ... shocked that you would want to do that. To *hurt* someone."

"They're not innocent, Mom."

"But ..." she trails off. "I don't even know what to think right now. I'm just ... disappointed."

And that hurts more than her being angry with me.

"Dad?" I ask.

He won't even look at me. "This is what I was talking about. I knew Luca would get you into dangerous situations. I just didn't realize he'd turn you into a monster like him."

"Hey, don't talk to my wife like that," Luca snaps. "Nat is amazing. I love the darkness inside her."

Dad stands up swiftly. "The darkness *you* brought out in her. She wouldn't be torturing men if it weren't for you. You're going to get my daughter killed one of these days, and then I'll murder you with my bare hands."

Luca stands up, too. They're the same height—eye to eye. "I'd be careful threatening me. You might not like the outcome."

"I have the full force of New York at my back, boy," Dad spits out. "You don't want to mess with me."

"Ok, enough," I say, joining them on my feet. "Enough of this alpha bullshit. Dad, I can make my own decisions. You blame Luca for how I act, but did you ever think that I choose to do things in life because I want to? Not because Luca is making me? And Luca,"—I shake my head at him—"I told you to be nice. And you just had to open your mouth."

"I was just stating a fact," Luca responds.

"A fact you knew would upset my parents. That isn't nice."

"Your parents should know the real you."

"And it was up to me to tell them!" I shout.

Luca takes a step back. "Nat ..."

"No. Just ... no. Not right now." I turn to my mom. "Mom? What are you thinking?"

She's staring down at her plate, not meeting my eyes. "I don't like you doing that. And it hurts me that you are."

"Please forgive me." My throat chokes up. "Please, Mom."

She finally looks at me. "Honey ..." She doesn't say anything else before she walks away. I've always had my mom on my side.

And now, I just lost her.

"You should go," Dad says tightly. "Before I do something I'll regret."

"Thanks for dinner," Luca says jovially as he saunters out of the room.

I can't believe this happened. I've lost my dad and my mom. I'm pissed at my husband. I've never felt this alone in my life before.

And it's all because of the decisions I've made.

"Dad?"

He lets out a rough breath, shaking his head. "Just don't let Luca get you hurt." With those words, he leaves me alone in the dining room.

After a moment, I follow Luca out of the house, even though all I want to do is stay.

CHAPTER 10
Natalya

Luca and I are silent on the car ride home. I can see him looking at me out of the corner of my eye, but I don't turn to him. Right now, I'm too angry.

Luca told my parents about what we've done, and while I never told Luca he couldn't tell them, I just assumed he wouldn't. It feels like he told them, knowing it would upset them, especially my dad. But what hurts even more is that my mom is disappointed in me for my actions. She was the real reason I didn't want them to know. While my dad and I have always had our difficulties, my mom and I have always been strong.

And now, I'm worried I've lost that. All because Luca couldn't keep his mouth shut even after I asked him to be nice and polite. He didn't listen to me. He's too caught up in pissing off my dad that I got caught in the crosshairs tonight.

When we get home, I immediately go to our room to change into pajamas, still ignoring Luca.

"Nat, baby, talk to me," he finally says as I slip off my dress. He reaches out for my waist, but I gently swat his hand.

"I'm not in the mood for that right now, Luca." I put on a cotton T-shirt and a pair of shorts.

"Then talk to me. Why are you mad at me?"

I give him a look. "Are you that obtuse? I know you're not. You told my parents about what we've done. How I've participated in torturing people with you."

He shrugs. "Why is that a problem? It's a part of you. You shouldn't be ashamed of it."

"Oh, I just shouldn't be ashamed that I've helped you hurt people? That I've *killed* a man for you?"

"No."

I huff. "You make it sound so simple. Luca, that darkness … Yes, it's a part of me. But my parents will never understand that. Maybe my dad can understand it, but he'll never be ok with me being like that. But my mom is one of the kindest, most compassionate people. She's a very forgiving person. But how can I expect her to understand what I've done when she can't even contemplate hurting an insect, let alone a human being?"

"Even if that human being deserves it?"

"Yes. Even then. She looked at me tonight like I was a stranger." Tears hit my eyes, and my throat chokes up. "All because you opened your mouth and told her."

"It's the truth, Nat. I'm not going to lie."

"But you only said it to piss off my dad!" I shout.

Luca blinks, looking surprised. I've never screamed at him like this before. Luca has only ever known my unconditional love. But tonight, he drew a line between my mom and me, and I'm not happy about it.

"Nat …"

I hold up a hand. "No. You know you said it to upset my dad. You love making him angry. You knew he wouldn't be ok with his daughter doing the things we've done together. You knew the minute you opened your mouth and said what you said that you would make my dad upset. So don't play innocent. Don't pretend you're just a great person who thinks honesty is the best policy when you had ulterior motives."

"Fine. You're right. But you know I'm not a good man. Don't pretend you're shocked to find this out. I showed you who I really was when I first killed Angelo." He points his finger at me. "And you showed me who you really are when you grabbed a bolt gun and shot him in the head. It doesn't matter that it didn't kill him. It doesn't matter that I'm the one who killed him. You still chose violence. I might have introduced you to it, but I've never forced you to partake in it."

"Oh, really?" I take a step toward him until there's barely any space left between us. "I remember when you told me that I had to choose between you or my family, and you said that if I wanted to prove myself to you, I'd have to kill a man. So, I did."

"But I never forced you," he growls. "I just gave you a choice."

"An impossible choice." I'm now fully realizing that.

"You're not innocent, Nat. Your parents should know that. I just opened their eyes to who you really are."

"But I never asked you to. You took it upon yourself without talking to me first. Without wondering how I'd feel about this. That's not ok, Luca."

He grabs my waist roughly. "You're only upset because you didn't like your parents' reaction. If they were fine with this, you'd have no problem."

"Don't blame this on me."

"Don't blame it on me, either."

We're breathing fast as we look at each other, our bodies so close. I can smell the wine on Luca's breath from here.

Suddenly, we're kissing. I'm not sure who did it first. Neither of us. Both of us. It's a battle between us, both of us trying to win, neither of us willing to lose.

When Luca pulls me tighter to him, I pull back. "We can't do this, Luca."

"What?" His eyes are dark and wild.

"I can't have sex with you right now. I'm too upset." I detangle myself from his arms.

"You're punishing me, huh?"

"It's not punishment, Luca. It's just how I feel. You don't get to distract me this time." I walk into the bathroom and shut the door, leaning my head against the cool wood. My body is singing for Luca, but my mind is in turmoil.

I've been so captivated by Luca ever since I met him that I never really thought how truly dangerous he could be. Sure, I've seen him torture and kill people, but that's not the danger that worries me.

He's already put a riff between me and my dad.

By speaking the truth, he's made a riff between my mom and me.

He's taking me away from my family and pulling me deeper and deeper into his dark world.

I believe *that's* the danger my father is always warning me about.

CHAPTER 11

Luca

Nat is distant from me. I know I fucked up at the family dinner, but I still stand by what I said. I believe her parents should know the truth about her, darkness and all.

Unfortunately, Nat doesn't see it that way. So, she's decided to punish me with no sex and no talking.

That's fine. I need to focus on Romeo anyway.

I've had an idea permeating for a while—ever since Romeo first declared war on me by grabbing Nat off the street.

I know Angelo had a daughter. That didn't impact me at all when I decided to kill him. He came after me and needed to die.

Now, Angelo's daughter is in Romeo's care. Which I know because I've been keeping my men on him. I never planned to get kids involved but plans change.

Romeo's niece—Isabella—is only four years old. If I take her, it will piss off Romeo, and he'll attack, giving me a chance to strike back and kill him.

I haven't told Nat my plan yet. With things being the way they are at the moment, she might not like my plan. I'm going to kidnap a four-year-old. Not my best moment in life, but you have to do what you have to do to win a war.

I leave Nat for the day, still sulking, as I head into work, where I put the plan into motion.

I go to work and wait for the call that Romeo has left his house. Once he does, I'll sneak in, grab Isabella, and take her to my home. I won't hurt the kid. I'll just keep her long enough for Romeo to do something stupid.

I spend time going through data sheets until I get the call. "He's left, sir," my guy Enzo tells me.

"Great." I inform my receptionist that I'll be leaving for the day, then drive to Romeo's house. Of course, he has guards everywhere. Which is why I came prepared with backup.

I call Enzo. "Ok. I'll take the guard out front and any others who get in my way. Back me up."

"You got it, sir."

I stroll up to Romeo's house like I own the place. The guard out front pauses then stands up straighter when he realizes who I am.

"Stop right there," he calls out.

I check to make sure no one else is on the street—it's empty—then pull my gun out and shoot him in the head. Thank god for silencers. The guard falls with a soft thud, dead. I step over him and keep walking.

Another guard comes running from the side, but Enzo, stationed in the building across the street with a rifle, shoots him. The guard falls next to his fallen comrade.

Even though I can't see Enzo from where I am, I nod toward the building he's in. Then, I keep moving.

I'm able to get inside the house with ease. My heart beats steadily, even though there's a thrill coursing through me. I love the hunt. It's the best thing about being in the mafia.

As I stalk through the house like I own it, a man comes racing out, firing a gun at me. I duck behind a wall. That was a close one.

Fortunately for me, I know what I'm doing. Unfortunately for the man, he's going to die.

"Come out, you bastard," the man snarls.

I just sigh as I look around the wall and fire, hitting him in the knee. He hits the ground hard, screaming profanities. I shoot him in the head. Silence. Thank fucking god. I was getting tired of his screaming.

No more guards come at me as I make my way up to Isabella's room. I've never been inside Romeo's house before—it's nice, if not a little outdated. Isabella's room is easy to find since it's the one covered in pink.

She's napping in her bed, with her brown hair spread across her pillow. Looking down at her, I can't help but think about how she reminds me of Nat. I wonder what Nat's and my children will look like. How innocent they'll be.

I nudge Isabella awake. She blinks her sleepy eyes open and stares at me in confusion. Interestingly, she's not afraid. She's too young to be afraid of a stranger. She's also probably used to the guards in her house. Maybe she thinks I'm one of them.

"Isabella, I'm a friend of your uncle. He sent me to take you to him."

She sits up, hugging her blanket to her chest. "What's the password?"

I blink. Of course. Romeo is smarter than I give him credit for. If I know the password, Isabella will trust me. The problem is—I don't know the fucking password.

I look around her room, taking in all the stuffed animals. On every shelf and every surface, there's a stuffed animal. But there's one in particular that stands out—most of the stuffed animals are giraffes.

It's worth a shot.

"Giraffe?"

A smile lights up her face. "Yeah!"

Lucky guess.

I smile back. "You can trust me, Isabella. My name is Luca. I'll take you to your uncle, but first, I'm going to take you somewhere, and you can have whatever you want."

"Ice cream?" she excitedly whispers.

"Yeah. You can have ice cream."

She hurries out of bed, making me chuckle. She holds out her hand for me to take, and I do. I've never felt the urge to be a father before, but at this moment, that's all I want to be. I want Nat and I to have kids someday, just as soon as she forgives me and we go back to having sex.

Isabella and I walk downstairs and out of Romeo's house without any other problems. She gets into the car without complaint, and off we go.

"Who's house is this?" she asks as I help her out of the car after we arrive at my house.

"It's mine. And you can have all the ice cream you want inside."

She practically runs to the door.

I let her inside and make good on my promise to get her ice cream. Isabella is contentedly eating ice cream on the couch when Nat enters the room and stops short.

"Um, Luca?"

I pull Nat away so Isabella can't overhear. "This is Isabella, Romeo's niece. Angelo's daughter."

Nat's eyes bulge out. "What is Romeo's niece doing in our house?"

I shrug. "I took her. Romeo is going to lose his mind when he finds out. I'll finally get a good shot at killing him."

"By kidnapping his niece?" Nat hisses. "Luca, I know you've done bad things. But … this is pretty low, even for you."

"I'm not going to hurt her. She'll just eat ice cream and relax until Romeo comes. Simple as that."

Nat shakes her head. "Luca, this is a horrible idea. She could get hurt in the process."

"She's not going to get hurt."

"How can you be so sure? I thought I was safe with you, and now, I'm not so sure."

Her words pull me up short. "You know you're safe with me, Nat."

She doesn't respond. She just walks into the living room and crouches beside Isabella, asking the four-year-old what her favorite ice cream is.

I just watch. How can Nat say she doesn't feel safe with me? I've done nothing but protect her.

Why do I feel that the chasm between us is growing bigger and bigger by the minute?

CHAPTER 12
Natalya

I stare into Isabella's innocent face as she eats ice cream. I can't believe Luca kidnapped a little girl. Or maybe I can. Luca is a dangerous man, I know. He's willing to do whatever he needs to take down Romeo.

Romeo took me, and now, Luca's taking something from Romeo.

But I just can't sit back and watch a little girl be used like this. It's not right. I may be ok with torturing bad men with Luca, but I'm not ok with innocent kids being involved.

"How old are you?" I ask Isabella.

"Four." She stuffs a huge spoonful of ice cream into her mouth. The result being ice cream dribbles down her chin. She doesn't even seem to care.

I stiffen. "You're only four," I mutter. I shoot a glare at Luca, who's in the doorway. He just shrugs and walks away.

I thought of Luca as this god. This otherworldly man who showed me what a future could be like. But the cracks are starting to form. Luca is looking more and more like a common man by the day, and it's disappointing.

My attention is drawn back to Isabella as she sets her bowl down. I need to get this kid out of here. It'll piss off Luca and might even give Romeo an advantage, but I can't just sit back and do nothing.

"Stay here," I tell her.

"Ok."

I go in search of Luca and find him in his office. "Luca, come on. This isn't ok. You need to give her back."

"I will give her back."

Hope flares in my chest. "Really?"

"Yes. Once Romeo discovers she's missing and comes after me. Once he's dead, I'll give her back."

"To who? You killed her dad, and now, you're going to kill her uncle."

Luca waves a dismissive hand. "She has other relatives, I'm sure. We're Italian. Most of us have a ton of relatives."

"What about you? You've never introduced me to all of your relatives."

He gives me a dark look. "That's because I don't have any."

"But you just said …" I shake my head. "Never mind. Luca, you have to give the girl back."

"She's part of my plan, so no."

"Kidnapping kids isn't good." I can't believe I even have to say that.

"I know it isn't. But my plan is for us. If I can draw Romeo out and get him to attack me, I'll have an easier time killing him."

"You managed to kidnap Isabella from her home, I'm guessing."

"Yes."

"So, then, why not just kill Romeo when you were there."

"Because I want him to hurt first."

I look away from him. Of course, he'd want that. He loves torturing people, after all. "Is this punishment for him taking me?"

"Yes. He thought he could just take you off the street, and there'd be no consequences. Well, he'll soon see the consequences."

"You won't change your mind, will you?"

Luca walks over to me, kissing me on the head. "Despite how

much I love you, your impassioned pleas mean nothing to me when it comes to this."

I flinch. Luca can be cold at times.

I return to the living room, where Isabella is napping on the couch. All that ice cream must've worn her out.

I'm taking her back.

I scoop her up, and she doesn't even wake up. Then I walk out the front door, careful to be quiet. I get in Luca's car and check to see where the last location is on his GPS. I just have to hope that's Romeo's house.

Starting the car, I pull into the road.

Luca comes running out of the house, staring at me with wide eyes, but I just keep driving.

It takes me around thirty minutes to get there. Isabella wakes up during that time, asking me what's going on. I tell her I'm taking her back to her uncle.

I reach a house so grand it's almost gaudy. I keep to the other side of the road, hoping Romeo won't see me.

"Is this your house?" I ask her. She nods. "Ok. Come on." I know it's a risk to walk her to the house, but I can't just let a four-year-old walk by herself.

Once we're out of the car, I hold her hand and walk her to the sidewalk in front of her home. "Can you get in?" I ask. There's no one outside. It's eerily quiet.

"I don't have a key," she says like I'm stupid for even asking.

"Ok." Dammit. I don't feel right just leaving her outside by herself, but what other choice do I have? Romeo could be back any minute, or he could be inside right now. He could see me and come after me. He did tell me that the next time he got his hands on me, he wouldn't let go.

"Just ... sit on your porch." I point toward the steps. Isabella does as she's told. "Ok. I'm going to get into my car, and once I do, you knock on your door. See if anyone is home, ok?"

She nods.

"Great." I'm hurrying across the street when Romeo's door opens. There he is.

"Isabella," he says, relief in his voice.

I start running toward my car, but then I hear him shout after me. After darting into the driver's seat, I scream as I shut my door because a bullet lodges itself in my window. Looking toward Romeo, I see he has a gun pointed in my direction. I don't see Isabella. She must be inside.

I gun the car and race away. It's only when I'm a few minutes away that I notice a car is following me. The person behind the wheel isn't trying to be subtle about it.

I speed up, and they do the same. Ok, ok. I need to be calm. I just need to get back home, and Luca will protect me.

But the car is inching dangerously close to me, almost on my bumper. I'm a few minutes from home now. I can do this. I can do this.

Then the car hits the back of my car, sending me bouncing forward. I grip the wheel tighter. I'm almost home. I'm almost home.

I get hit again, this time harder. I almost lose control of my car, but I manage to righten it.

Turning down a street, I see my house. The car behind me speeds up and slams into mine, causing me to crash into a lamppost. I scream as the car smashes into the pole, shards from the window shattering around me.

I need to get out of this car. I try opening the door, but it's stuck.

A man gets out of the car behind me—not Romeo. A guard of his, perhaps. He stalks toward me, a gun in his hand.

I scramble to get out the passenger side, but I'm too late. He's at the driver's door, pointing his gun at me.

I squeeze my eyes shut, bracing myself for death …

… when a gunshot goes off.

But I'm not dead. I'm not even hurt.

I open my eyes. The man isn't there anymore. Instead, I see Luca pointing a gun in my direction. He lowers it and comes running toward me.

"Luca," I gasp as he opens the passenger door and helps me out. He wraps me in his arms. It's the safest place I can be at the moment.

When we walk around the car, I see the man's dead body lying on the street, a bullet hole in his head.

"Luca." My voice comes out as a sob. He helps me into the house.

"Nat, are you hurt?" He rakes his eyes over me, searching for any injuries.

"I'm fine. Just … in shock, I think."

He grabs his phone and calls someone. "Yeah. I need you to come to dispose of a body. At my house." He hangs up. "Nat, what were you thinking? You brought Isabella back to Romeo?"

"I did. He saw me. He tried shooting at me, but I was already in the car. Then he sent a man to follow me."

"Fuck." Luca rakes his hands through his hair. "This was not how it was supposed to go. I didn't want you getting hurt. Never put yourself in danger like that again."

"You brought danger into our house when you kidnapped a four-year-old, Luca."

"And you gave her back. Now, my plan is fucked. Romeo will have no reason to come over here and get his niece back. You gave away my bargaining chip!" he screams at me.

He's never screamed at me before.

I flinch in fear, curling inward.

Luca blinks. "Nat … I'm …"

"I'm just going to lie down. I'm pretty tired." I walk out of the room and toward our bedroom.

Luca doesn't follow.

CHAPTER 13

Luca

I'm pissed.

Not only did Nat go against my plan, but she also could have died in the process.

I give her the night to sleep since I know she went through a lot. Now that it's morning, I'm ready to tell her how upset I am with her.

I'm waiting in the kitchen for her when she comes downstairs. "Nat, we need to talk."

She gets a glass of water and takes a sip. "What's there to talk about? You kidnapped a little girl. I brought her back. Almost died. You saved me. There we go."

"You went against my plan. How could you do that?"

"Maybe because I'm a grown woman with a mind of my own. I don't follow you blindly, Luca." She sits down across from me, defiance in her eyes. Honestly, it's fucking sexy. It makes me want to jump across this table and fuck her.

"You fucked up my plan," I growl.

"That's all you care about?"

"I care that you almost died. That's what upsets me the most. I could've lost you, all because you didn't listen to me. And not only that, but you ruined any advantage I had over Romeo. You delivered his niece right back to him."

"Because she's a four-year-old. She didn't need to be involved in the first place. That was wrong of you to do."

"We've both committed murder. How is that ok and kidnapping a kid is not?"

Her mouth gapes open. "You're seriously asking me that."

"I am."

"Well, for one, we've only hurt people who deserved it. An innocent kid doesn't deserve this."

"You're just assuming I've only hurt bad people. I'm a mafia boss, baby. You should know better by now that I'm capable of anything."

"I'm realizing that, yes. And I hate this side of you. You're becoming too consumed by Romeo."

"Because I don't want him to kill you."

"I understand that, but the Luca I knew before wouldn't have involved a child in his plans."

"Then I guess you don't know me very well. I'm a ruthless son-of-a-bitch. I've never claimed not to be. This is me, Nat. I won't let Romeo hurt you. But don't get in the way of my plans again."

She crosses her arms. "Or what? What are you going to do to me?"

I stare at her for a moment, breathing heavily. She has a way of riling me up. I can't take it any longer.

I get up and stalk toward her. Nat's eyes widen, but she doesn't move.

Grabbing the back of her head, I lean down and kiss her. Nat responds immediately, clutching my back, a soft moan escaping her. I kiss her so deeply it's like we become one.

Then I lift Nat and sit her on the table, squeezing her waist.

"Luca," she gasps as I kiss down her neck. She wraps her legs around my waist, drawing me closer.

In a frenzy, we tear at each other's clothes. Nat's dress is around her waist, allowing me to lavish her breasts with attention. She moans, dropping her head back while gripping the back of my head.

Her fingers undo my belt buckle. When she reaches into my pants and touches my cock, I feel like I might burst right then and there.

I trail kisses back up to her lips as I shove her dress around her waist and tear her panties off. Nat opens her legs wider, and I place my cock against her entrance.

Our eyes meet. We're both breathing heavily.

It's Nat who grabs my waist and pulls me in closer. As I enter her, we moan in unison.

Our hands grip each other's backs as we fuck with a frenzied passion that almost makes me afraid.

"Fuck. Nat. God, I love you," I say into her ear.

"Luca." She leans back on the table, pleasure written all over her face. She's perfect like this. "I love you."

My hips grind against hers. My lips mold with hers. My hands twine with hers.

"You're mine," I tell her. "You're always mine."

"Always," she gasps as she comes. Her inner walls clench tight onto my cock, pushing me over the edge.

I groan into her neck as my orgasm hits me.

It's only when we're done trembling that we pull apart.

I cup her cheek. "I only want to protect you."

Her eyes soften as she leans into my hand. "I know."

I LEAVE Nat with a guard when I go to work for the day. Maybe things will be ok between us. They have to be. She's my wife. The woman I love. It has to be.

But things aren't looking up when I get a call from Romeo. "You took my niece," he growls.

I have to resist laughing. "Of course I did. You tried to take my wife. It's only payback. I needed you to know not to mess with me."

"I saw your pretty wife here last night. I'm shocked you're getting your wife to do your dirty work."

"Well, she's a good one." I can't admit to Romeo that Nat went against my plans. That will only serve to make me look weak.

"She sure is. I'm looking at her right now."

I sit upright in my seat. "You're at my house?"

"Of course, I am. You knew I'd retaliate. That's why you took Isabella to begin with. Now, I'm taking your wife as I promised I would."

"You fucker."

"Tit-for-tat, Luca." He hangs up.

I rush out of the building and to my car, driving like a madman all the way home. When I get there, I see the guard I had watching Nat dead in the foyer. Jack. He was one of the best. Romeo must have brought a lot of men with him to overpower Jack.

I look over every inch of my house but don't see Nat anywhere.

She's gone.

CHAPTER 14
Natalya

Romeo came in into my house like an explosion—killing the guard, Jack, who was watching me, and grabbing me within a matter of a few seconds. He came with a large group of men, so Jack didn't stand a chance.

Now, I'm at Romeo's house.

I'm in the kitchen, tied to a chair, watching Romeo pace back and forth. "You didn't have to do this," I tell him.

"I did. Luca thinks he can come after me? This will show him."

"But I'm the one who brought Isabella back. I wasn't ok with Luca doing that. Don't punish me for his crimes."

He snorts. "I seriously doubt you'd go against your husband. No. This was somehow part of his plan. I just need to figure it out."

"I already told you. I made the decision to bring Isabella back. This was *not* Luca's plan."

"It's cute how you think that."

God. I want to drive a knife right into Romeo's chest. "I have a mind of my own, you know."

"Sure you do."

Oh, for god's sake. Fine. If Romeo wants to think I'm a mindless idiot, then let him. Maybe I can use it to my advantage.

"You know, you're right," I say. Romeo looks proud of himself for this. "It was Luca's plan for me to bring Isabella back. In fact, it was his plan for you to take me and bring me here. He's coming for you, Romeo. He knows I'm here. He'll kill you when he comes for me."

He stops pacing. "I'm hoping he does exactly that. I have a plan for him in mind."

"So does my husband. He won't risk me getting hurt."

"Are you so sure about that? He used you in his plan. I could have killed you yesterday, but, I'll admit, I missed. I'm happy I did, though. You're face is too pretty for it to be lifeless."

I know Luca will come for me. We might be going through a slight rough patch, but we love each other. We're obsessed with each other. Luca only wants to protect me.

I am pissed at him, though. He's the reason we're in this mess. He's the one who killed Angelo. He's the one who kidnapped Isabella, bringing danger to our doorstep. He's the reason I've been kidnapped. Romeo doesn't want me. He wants Luca, and I'm a pawn for him to get my husband.

My dad was right, I realize. Luca put me in danger. He's reckless and wild and doesn't consider the outcomes of his actions. He truly thought I'd be safe, and now look where I am.

"What are you going to do with me?"

Romeo leans in close to me. His breath smells like alcohol—I hate it. "After I kill Luca, I'm going to keep you." He runs a finger down my cheek. "We're going to have fun together. But until then, you're going to stay tied to this chair, looking pretty." He leans back, giving me a chance to breathe.

"Uncle Romeo," Isabella's voice comes out soft as she runs into the kitchen. She stops short when she sees me.

"Isabella, you're not supposed to be in here," Romeo snaps at her.

A woman enters the room, looking out of breath. "Sorry, sir. She ran away from me. I couldn't stop her."

"She's four. You can stop her. Keep her in her room for now."

The woman nods, grabbing Isabella's hand. "Come on, young lady."

Isabella continues to look at me as she leaves the room. I wonder what she's thinking. I'm tied to a chair. She can't understand why, I'm sure. She's too young. I feel bad that she has to grow up in this world.

Then I remember—*I've* grown up in this world. Even though my dad protected me from it, I was still close to it. That's one difference between my dad and Luca. My dad raised me for twenty years, and I didn't know about the dangers of the world he inhabited.

But being with Luca for less than a year, I'm already shrouded in darkness and danger.

I love my husband, and I trust him to come for me. But I'm learning that my dad was right to warn me about him. That's a sad thought.

"You're going to stay here," Romeo says as he grabs a rag off the counter. "And you're going to stay quiet." He stuffs the rag into my mouth. I gag. "When Luca comes for you, I'll be ready for him."

He leaves the room. I'm all alone. That's how little Romeo thinks of me. But I can use that to my advantage.

I'm getting out of here.

CHAPTER 15
Natalya

It's been over an hour, and no one has checked on me. I look around the kitchen, searching for signs of a camera that may be watching me, but there are none.

Romeo truly doesn't think I can escape. That, or this is a test. But even if it is, I'm not waiting around to get hurt.

As I've waited, I've been working at the knots on the rope around my wrists. Though, it hasn't been easy since I have to contort my wrist in an awkward, uncomfortable position to reach the knots. A sharp pain keeps slicing up my forearm. But I keep working on them.

I won't stop until I've undone them.

I'm breathing heavily, my fingers are getting cramped and achy, and my heart is racing. Romeo could return at any moment.

My finger feels like it might break in half as I try to untie the knot. It hurts so bad. I grit my teeth and keep pushing through. I can do this. I am strong.

I am Luca's wife, after all.

The things I've been through … I can handle a knot.

I gasp when the rope slackens around my wrists. I pull my hands around, throw the rope away, then rub my wrists. Red welts are already forming on my skin.

I quickly untie my ankles and get up.

Now, what?

If I make a run for it, Romeo could catch me. Maybe he's waiting for me already.

Or I could d hide and hope Luca shows up. I know Luca will show up. That's exactly what Romeo wants, which means he has a plan for Luca. I just don't know what it is yet.

But first things first ... I need a weapon.

I grab the biggest knife I can find from the butcher block. It's larger than my forearm. This will do some damage if I get caught.

Taking a deep breath, I begin to walk out of the kitchen. Peering into the hallway, I don't see anyone. I don't hear anyone, either. What's Romeo's plan?

I can see the front door at the end of the hall. I can easily run for it, but it almost seems too good to be true.

I don't have any other options, so I decide to go for it.

I run with all my might to the front door, but when I go to open it, heavy footsteps come up behind me. I spin around and jab the knife into ...

Romeo.

He steps back, shocked. The knife is sticking out of his shoulder, which means I didn't hit any vital organs. "Where do you think you're going?" he asks, frowning at the knife.

"You left me alone. What do you think I would do? Just sit still."

"Yes. That's exactly what I thought you would do."

"Then you don't know me very well." I turn the knob, but the door doesn't open. It's locked.

Romeo begins laughing. "You'd really thought it would be that easy to escape?"

A red-hot anger passes over me. I grab the knife and pull it out of his shoulder. He groans, stumbling back. Blood begins to seep down his arm.

"Don't mess with me," I warn.

He clamps his hand onto his wound, glaring at me as he responds, "You bitch."

I jerk the knife forward and slice Romeo across his face.

He growls as he rushes me and grabs the knife from my hand. He throws it down the hallway. "Enough of this." Pulling out a gun, he presses it to my head.

I stop.

"Now, you wanna be good?" He pushes the gun harder against my temple. "Why don't you sit back down and wait for Luca to arrive like the good girl you are."

"My husband will kill you," I hiss.

"I'd like to see him try." Romeo walks me back to the chair in the kitchen and ties me to it again. "There. Now, just sit pretty as we wait for your husband's arrival." Romeo grabs a rag and presses it to his wound. Then he gets duct tape from a drawer and uses it to keep the rag in place. I like the look of pain on his face. Serves him right for kidnapping me.

Romeo then sits beside me, pointing his gun at me. "Now, we wait."

Fortunately, we don't have to wait long for Luca to arrive. I know the moment he does because the front door bangs open, and Luca's voice fills the house.

"Romeo!" he shouts. "Where the fuck are you?"

"In here," Romeo calls out.

Luca comes into the kitchen and stops short when he sees me tied up with a gun to my head. "Nat."

"I'm ok," I tell him.

"Your little wife is a lot feistier than I gave her credit for," Romeo cuts in. I shoot him a glare. "If you shoot me, Luca, there's a good chance your wife dies with me."

Luca lowers his gun. "Let her go. This fight is between you and me."

"I know. But I just want you dead." In a flash, Romeo turns his gun onto Luca and fires. Luca manages to jump out of the way, but I notice he doesn't fire back. He doesn't want to risk shooting me in the process.

I shift in my seat until the chair tips to the side, and I fall to the ground. It knocks the wind out of me, but it puts me out of the line of danger.

Romeo continues firing after Luca while Luca hides behind the wall. I know he's waiting for his opportunity to strike. I just need to be out of the way.

Then I get an idea.

Romeo is standing in front of me. Using all my strength, I kick him in the back of the shin, making him cry out and stumble.

Luca uses this to his advantage. He leans out from behind the wall and fires, but Romeo shifts just in time, so he's only shot in the arm, not the head. He fires again, forcing Luca to duck out of the way. Romeo keeps shooting until he's run out of bullets. His eyes widen.

We both know what that means.

Luca will kill him.

Romeo turns heel and runs out of the kitchen through the back entrance. Luca curses and starts to chase after Romeo when he stops and looks down at me.

"Go after him," I tell Luca.

Luca looks in the direction Romeo went before making a face and turning back to me. "No. I can't leave you here. I can't risk you getting hurt. I need to get you out." He unties me from the chair and helps me stand up.

And then, together, we hurry out of the house.

Once we're in his car, I turn to him and say, "That was your chance to get him."

"Not at the expense of you. There'll be other chances." He speeds away from Romeo's house.

"Damnit, Luca!"

"What? Are you mad at me? I saved you, Nat!"

"I know you did. But Romeo is still out there. He's going to come back, and he's going to keep coming back. You should have gone after him."

"I couldn't let you get hurt. I had to save you."

"I didn't ask you to! I told you to go after him, and you didn't listen."

He grips the steering wheel tighter. "I'm not going to apologize for saving you."

"But you're the reason I was in that position to begin with!" I've never yelled at Luca like this before.

"Oh, so all of this is my fault?"

"You kidnapped Romeo's niece. You were asking for trouble. You killed Angelo, not giving any thought to his brother who might come after you. I asked you to be smart about Romeo and not bring trouble to our doorstep, but you didn't listen. Romeo kidnapped me in retaliation for the things you did. So, yes. I have the right to blame you."

Luca scoffs. "I just saved you, and this is the thanks I get?"

"You're not hearing me, Luca."

"Oh, I am." He raises his voice. "You knew I was dangerous when we met. You knew who you were marrying. Don't blame all of this on me."

"I never thought I'd be hurt because of your actions, but here we are. I'm fucking angry with you."

Luca is silent. The only reason I know he's angry is because it radiates off every inch of him.

"My dad was right," I murmur. "He warned me that you'd put me in danger."

"Don't you dare say that," he growls. "Don't you fucking say your dad was right."

"But he was. I was just kidnapped by some crazy guy because you've started a war with him. I've gotten hurt, Luca. And it was because of you. This is the first time I've ever been disappointed by you." I look out the window, focusing on the other cars driving past.

I can't bear to see the look of hurt on his face.

Because while Luca has hurt me, I know what I'm doing with my words. I want him to hurt in the same way.

CHAPTER 16
Natalya

Luca and I aren't speaking. It's been a couple of days, and we're stuck in a stalemate.

So, I decide to go to my parents' house. There are some things we need to talk about.

I go with the new guard Luca has assigned me—Robot. He's quiet and doesn't bother me. Nor does his presence offer me much comfort after the last guard who kept an eye on me—Jack—was killed by Romeo.

After I knock, my dad answers. The minute he sees me, he pulls me into a hug. It startles me at first, but then I sink into his arms.

"Dad, what was that for?"

He shuts the door behind me, leaving Robot outside. "I heard about how Romeo kidnapped you. I had men out looking for you, but Luca found you. I was told you were all right."

Mom comes rushing down the stairs to hug me, too. "I'm so glad you're all right."

"I am. I am. Why didn't either of you call?" I look between them.

They both look ashamed.

"After our last talk …" Mom begins. "I wasn't sure if you'd be happy to hear from us."

"Of course, I'd be happy. I've regretted how things were left between us. You were disappointed in me."

"I know I said that," she says. "But ... I've missed you, honey. I'm tired of us not talking. I'm not happy about what Luca told us, but I'm willing to listen to what you have to say about the matter."

"Let's sit down." Dad leads us into the living room, where we settle into our seats. Mom and me on the couch. Dad in the armchair. It's such a familiar scene it almost makes my heart ache. I've missed my parents, too. I hate this strained tension between us.

"First," Mom starts. "You're all right?"

"I am. Romeo kidnapped me, but he didn't touch me. Luca got to me before anything happened."

"Good." Mom looks relieved. "I was so worried when we found out. I told your dad to rescue you. He was out there looking for you."

I turn to him. "You were?"

He sets his intense blue eyes on me. "Of course, I was. You're my daughter. I didn't know where Romeo had you, but I wasn't going to stop until I knew you were safe."

His words warm my heart. "He had me at his house. Luca knows where it is. He didn't call you to let you know?"

"No. My men told me you'd been taken, but they lost sight of Romeo, so they couldn't save you."

"Good thing for Luca," Mom adds.

My mood instantly sours. "It's partly his fault I was taken. He kidnapped Romeo's niece to get Romeo to attack him so Luca could kill him, but I wasn't comfortable having a child used in this war, so I brought her back. But Romeo saw me and came after me in retaliation for Luca taking his niece. Luca is getting out of control. I told him he needs to be smart about this, but he's not listening."

"You're mad at him," Dad states, like he knew this was coming all along. And I guess he sort of did.

"I am," I admit. "But he did save me. And I know he just wants me to be ok. But ..." I inhale deeply and let it out slowly. I have to say this. "You were right."

Dad barely reacts to my words. He's his cool, calm self, as always. "How so?"

As I bow my head, Mom rubs my knee. "Luca is dangerous, and it's gotten me into trouble. His recklessness put me at risk."

"Why are you telling me this?" he asks.

"Because I needed to say it. And it hurts me to say it. So, don't tell me 'I told you so,' ok? I don't think I'd be able to handle it."

"I wasn't going to. I knew you'd see the truth eventually."

"I love him, Dad. That won't change. You need to know that."

He lets out a deep sigh. "I know."

"But I'm tired of this wall between us. I miss you," I whisper. "Can't we go back to the way things were before?" It startles me when I feel tears prick my eyes.

Dad stares at me a moment before getting up and wrapping me into another hug. "Yes. And … I'm sorry I pushed you away. That wasn't the right thing for me to do."

I cry into his chest. "I just needed to become my own person."

"I know."

We hold each other for a while. Mom looks on, a smile on her face.

When we finally pull back, all I want to do is sink into the safety of my father's arms again. It reminds me of how safe I felt as a child. I don't feel that same level of safety now.

"I love you, Natalya. I always will. And I'll never push you away like I did before."

"I love you, too, Dad."

He clears his throat. It takes me a moment to realize he's pushing back tears. "I know you're mad at Luca right now, but I'm partly to blame for this. If I hadn't pushed you away, I could have kept you safe. Maybe I could have stopped Romeo from kidnapping you if I'd had a better eye on you."

"It's not your fault, Dad. I decided to be with Luca. And I don't regret it. But I'm starting to realize that you were right to warn me about him."

"Do you want me to talk to him?"

"No," I say quickly. "It'll only rile him up. I need Luca calm right now before he does something stupid again. It'll get figured out. It just makes me happy to have you back in my life."

I turn to Mom. "And I want to explain more about what Luca said that night at dinner."

"I'm listening," she says.

"You raised me to be compassionate. But Luca woke up something inside me that is ... darker. And I know it's not what you want to hear. But I've helped him torture people."

Both my parents look uncomfortable at my confession.

"At first,"—I continue—"I was scared. But then it started to feel right. He's only ever had me join him when it comes to people who are vile. People who are ... not good. And I think part of this darkness comes from Dad."

"Something else I am at fault for," he says.

"I'm just saying I'm a combination of the two of you. Mom's compassion, and ... Dad's darkness. I don't want to see innocent people or animals hurt. But I have no qualms about seeing someone who's terrible get what they deserve. And that's where I stand. I hope you can accept me for that." I sit up straighter, waiting for them to express their disappointment again.

Mom takes my hand. "I understand."

"You do?"

She nods. "I know what it's like to want a bad person to hurt. There was this man who kidnapped you when you were a baby."

"I never knew this."

"I never wanted you to know. But you need to know." Mom sucks in a shaky breath. This is hard on her.

"You don't have to, Katia," Dad cuts in.

"No. I want to talk about." She readies herself. "This man, Mikhail, kidnapped you as a baby. Right after I gave birth to you, actually. It was the scariest moment of my life. Your dad went after him, and ... I went with him. He didn't want me to, but nothing would stop me from going after you. So, I was there ... when your dad killed him. I didn't stop it. I didn't want to stop him. So, I understand that darkness. When someone does something terrible, you want them to pay for it. While I might not agree with your torturing people … as long as they aren't innocent, I'll try not to be too bothered by it."

"Thank you."

She kisses my hand. "Of course."

I turn to Dad. "And what do you think about this?"

"I've been trying to protect you all my life. I saw you as this precious little being. But you're more like me than I thought. I'm not sure if that's a good thing or not."

"You've done dark things, but you're not a bad person, Dad. You've shown me love throughout my life. You're strong. And brave. You lead this city like it's nothing. If I can even be a little bit like you, then that's a pretty accomplished feat. So, no. I don't think it's a bad thing."

He smiles.

I look between my parents and know that things are turning out for the better. It gives me hope that Luca and I will be all right, too.

CHAPTER 17
Luca

I have another plan to take down Romeo since the little weasel keeps escaping my clutches. The only problem is that I need to tell Nat since she'll want to know, and currently, we're not speaking.

She's still angry with me about Romeo. I don't understand why. This is war. You have to do things in a war to win. And I'm not the one who kidnapped Nat. Romeo did. I'm the one who saved her, and she can't seem to understand that. I'm on her side, yet she's insisting *I'm* the reason we're in this mess in the first place.

I get home from work to find Nat gone. For a moment, I think she's been taken again, but then I find a note on the kitchen table telling me she went to see her parents. I relax a little but almost immediately tense back up. Nat went to her parents, which means she'll come back crying, or I can expect Alek will come bursting through my front door, ready to fight me again.

I sit on the couch, waiting for her to return.

When I hear the front door open, I brace myself for whatever will happen next. But what I see surprises me. Nat looks … happier. More relaxed.

"Hi," I say, standing up.

She blinks in surprise before sighing and walking closer to me. "Hi."

"I got your note."

"Yeah. I needed to talk to my parents, and it was a good thing. We cleared the air. Things are ... better."

"That's good." All I want to do is grab her and kiss the fuck out of her. But there's still this wall between us that I feel like I can't climb over.

"And it made me think that ... things can improve for us, too."

"You think that?" Hope flares in my heart.

"I do. Just as long as you end things with Romeo. This war can't last forever."

"I know. Which is why I've come up with another plan to go after Romeo."

"Oh?" I notice she tenses slightly.

"Romeo runs a cocaine shipping business. He and Angelo did. I'm going to bust it. Have the cops come and arrest him."

"Not kill him?"

I shrug. "Once he's in prison, it won't be hard to hire someone to kill him. I figured this would be a better alternative than getting you involved."

"I'm touched, Luca, but ..."

"But?" I lean against the couch. "But what? It's a good plan."

"But you'd have to make sure Romeo is there when the bust goes down."

"I know. I'll be there to make sure it happens."

"But couldn't that put you at risk? What if the police arrest you, too?"

"Your dad owns half the police force. He could do me a favor."

"I think you're asking too much from my dad."

"True." I place my hands on her shoulders. It feels fucking amazing to touch her again, even a simple gesture like this. "But I'll be fine. Romeo will go down. This war will end. Things will go back to normal."

"I just feel like this is dangerous, getting the police involved. I assumed you mafia men would hate that."

"I do hate the police. But I can't think of another way to get rid of Romeo that doesn't involve you getting hurt."

"But *you* could get hurt. You could get arrested, and then I'd be without you."

"I also could have gotten shot many times, and I've survived. I doubt a few measly police offers can take me down."

She looks away from me. "I just … I don't know."

"I thought you'd be happy I was going this route instead of getting involved in a shootout with Romeo."

"No, I am. I just feel like … something could easily go wrong. What if the police don't catch Romeo? Then you have the police involved in your life, and Romeo is still out there. You said it yourself—the police won't catch you. So, if you think they're that incompetent, then why would they catch Romeo?"

"Because Romeo isn't me. He's a fool. He'll get caught."

"I think you underestimate him."

"I think I know Romeo better than you do."

She steps away from me. "Fine. Do whatever you want. I just want this war to end." She walks away before I can tell her when this will take place.

I'm going after Romeo tomorrow night. I'll end things once and for all.

CHAPTER 18

Natalya

I'm worried for Luca. I just think getting the police involved is asking for trouble. Even if he manages to take down Romeo, what if this plan sends even more men after us? Luca and I may never have a moment's piece.

So, that's why I've come up with my own plan. It's one last desperate attempt to squash this.

I'm going to Romeo myself and asking him to back off before things go too far.

There's a good chance he won't listen to me, but I have to try. I can't see Luca get hurt.

So, when Luca's at work, I go to Romeo's house with the guard, Robert.

"Are you sure about this?" he asks as we pull up.

"No. But I'll have you with me. Keep me safe."

He nods.

I'm trembling as I get out of the car and approach Romeo's house. A guard out front puts his hand up. "Stop right there. What are you doing here?"

"I need to talk to Romeo. It's urgent."

The guard looks between Robert and me. "Only if you go in by yourself."

"No. My guard stays with me. Romeo can understand that. I have some information he'll want to hear, so I suggest he come out here if he wants to hear it."

He grumbles under his breath before pulling out his phone. "Yeah, boss? Luca's wife is out here to see you. I don't know what she wants." He puts his phone away. "He'll be out in a minute."

I stand there awkwardly, waiting for Romeo to arrive. When he finally does, I feel the breath leave my body. He could easily kidnap me again, but I'm hoping he'll back off when I tell him what I know.

"What do you want?" he asks.

"I'm here to ask that you stop this war with Luca."

He snorts. "Now, why the hell would I do that? He's trying to kill me."

"Only because you tried to kill him first."

"Semantics. If that's all you had to say to me, girl, you're best on your way." He approaches me, his gaze darkening. "Unless, of course, you want to stay here with me."

I crinkle up my nose. "Never."

He laughs. "Then, leave." He turns away from me.

"Luca is going to set the cops on your next cocaine shipment."

That makes him pay attention. "What? When?"

"I don't know when. I just know he's going to do it. And the only reason I'm telling you this is, so you understand how far my husband is willing to take things. If you stop pursuing him, he'll back off."

"You just gave away your husband's plan. How stupid are you?"

"I just want this war to end. If you don't want your next shipment spoiled by the police, I suggest you back off, too. Leave my husband and me alone."

"Never," he snarls, grabbing my arm.

Robert has his gun out instantly, pointing at Romeo's head. But then Romeo's guard has his weapon out, directed at Robert's head.

"You're coming with me," Romeo tells me, walking me to his car.

"Stop," Robert threatens. "Or I'll shoot."

Romeo shrugs. "Then my man will just kill you. If you want to protect Natalya, then you best get in line." He pushes me into his car, and after hesitating, Robert joins me in the car. Romeo takes his gun from him. Romeo's guard gets in, and all four of us head somewhere unknown.

"Was this part of your plan?" Robert whispers to me.

"No."

After a while, we wind up near the docks, parked in front of a warehouse. Romeo leads me inside, and what I see makes me gasp. Rows up rows of blocks of cocaine sit on tables. A row of men are cutting it and putting it into the blocks.

"Your drug shipment," I murmur.

"Heads up, boys!" Romeo shouts. "We need to get out of here now." He turns to me. "You better be telling me the truth about your husband's plan. I don't want to have to waste any good product."

"I am. By giving you this information, I ask that you leave Luca and me alone. I just did you a massive favor. Now, you have time to get this out of here before any police show."

As if on cue, sirens ripple through the air.

I blanche.

Romeo glares at me. "Did me a favor, huh? You just brought me here so I'd get caught."

"No, honestly. I didn't know when Luca would be sending the police."

"Fucking bitch. Men!" he shouts. "We need to get out of here now. Just run." Chaos spreads through the room as the men take off in different directions. The sirens are getting closer.

I start to run when Romeo grabs my arm. "Where do you think you're going?"

"Let go of me," I grit out, trying to break away from him, but Romeo has too tight of a hold on me.

"Let her go," Robert warns.

Romeo grabs his gun and shoots Robert in the head.

I gasp. I would have fallen back if not for Romeo's hand on my arm.

"You brought me here," Romeo says, raising his gun to my head. "You try to act all innocent like you're not just as bad as your husband. But you are. You are."

I squeeze my eyes shut, bracing myself for the pain, when I hear a loud sound. A bang. I open my eyes to see the warehouse doors swinging open and a collective of police busting in.

"Shit," Romeo hisses. He pushes me into the table full of cocaine and takes off running.

I hit the table so hard it knocks the wind out of me. I can't move for a moment. But by then, it's too late.

I'm the only one left in a room full of cocaine.

A police officer approaches me with a gun in his hands. "Hands on your head," he shouts at me.

Oh no. Oh no. Shit.

I do as the officer says, and he roughly pushes me to the ground. I cry out, but my cries are ignored. It's commotion around me. The police are raiding the warehouse. The officer is reading me my rights as he handcuffs me.

I'm getting arrested.

How far I've fallen.

CHAPTER 19
Natalya

It all happens so fast.
    I'm in the back of a police car. I'm taken to the nearest police station. I'm fingerprinted. My mugshot is taken.

And lastly, I'm put in a holding cell. It's dark and cold, with only a bench on one side. It's also crowded with people. The other women range in appearance. Some are young, some old. Some look like they could kill me with their fingernails. Some look messy. Some look clean-cut. This is a New York police station. I guess there are many different types of people in a place like this.

Including me.

I move into a less crowded corner and keep to myself. I'm not supposed to be here. I wasn't supposed to be at the drug bust. I had no idea when Luca would be making that call.

My guess, he had men watching for when Romeo showed up. I just wasn't a part of that plan.

I wonder if Luca knows. He must, surely. He's probably so angry with me for going against his wishes and getting arrested. And honestly? I deserve it. I've killed a man, after all. I've probably committed the worst crime here among all these women, yet, I'm the most innocent looking in my clean dress and smooth hair. How ironic.

"What are you in for?" A woman with long dirty blonde hair sidles up to me. She has a hippie vibe going on.

"Drugs," is all I say.

She nods, understanding in her eyes. "Same. Got busted with heroin before I could take it. Fuckers." She rubs her arms. I can see the track marks in them. "I need another fix. Do you have anything?"

"Uh, no."

Her kind look immediately shifts to annoyance. "Bitch," she mutters before walking away.

I turn inward on myself. These women are not my friends. I just need to focus on getting out of here.

A fight between two women breaks out, causing chaos in the cell.

"Enough," one officer says as he approaches the cell. "Natalya Romano?"

I hurry to the front. "That's me."

"You can make a phone call." He lets me out of the cell and leads me to the phone.

I immediately start dialing Luca's number when I stop half-way through. I can't face Luca. I went against his plan, trying to make things better, and I only made them worse. Hopefully, Romeo was caught by the police, but I didn't personally see it. I was too busy being handcuffed to notice.

Luca will be so disappointed in me. I can't handle that. Not right now.

No, right now, I need someone I can depend on. Someone who's the most powerful man in all of New York.

I dial my dad's number. "Dad?" I ask after he picks up. "I need your help."

CHAPTER 20

Luca

I'm awaiting news about the results of my plan.
I had men watching Romeo's house, and they told me when he arrived at his warehouse full of cocaine. Another of my men called in an anonymous tip to the police. I can only hope they caught the bastard, and then I can have him killed in prison.

Nat and I will be fine. I'll make sure of it.

But the minute Alek Antonov bursts into my office, I know something is wrong.

"Dad," I say.

He grabs my shirt and pushes me against the wall. My receptionist, Sarah, comes running in.

"It's ok," I tell her. After she leaves, I say to my father-in-law, "Alek. What's going on? Last I checked, I hadn't done anything recently to piss you off."

"Natalya is in jail."

My breath leaves my body. "What?"

"She called me. She told me about your plan for Romeo. How you sent the cops to take him down. But she was there with him. She got caught. Now, I need to make sure she's safe. I only came here to let you know since you're her husband." He shoves me before letting me go. "I figured you'd want to come with."

"Wait. Stop. Why was Nat with Romeo?"

"Because she was trying to stop this pointless war between you two. She got caught in the crosshairs. You were supposed to deal with Romeo, and you didn't."

"Did Romeo get taken by the police, too?"

"Natalya said she saw him escape, but who knows."

"Fuck," I mutter, running a hand through my hair. "I have to go save her. She needs me." I take one step, but Alek blocks my path.

"She called me. She wants my help. You better not fuck up again."

"Why didn't she call me?" I try to hide my hurt, but I'm sure it's written all over my face.

"She doesn't trust you."

"Did she say that?"

"She didn't have to. I could hear it in her voice. Because of your plan, she's now in danger. I'm going to get her out. You can either stay or come with."

"You know I'm coming. She's my wife."

"Well, she's my daughter."

We pause, glaring at each other in a standoff.

I realize it's up to me to make any difference with Alek. He doesn't trust me and probably never will. I can't expect him to budge.

"Once we get Nat out … will you help me stop Romeo?"

"You asked before."

"I know I did. And you didn't want to help. You said it was my problem to deal with. But look how that turned out. I tried dealing with it, and now, Nat's in prison. Let's work together. For real, this time. No more having me run errands for you. Let's stand as equals. Let's make ourselves so strong that Nat will never be at risk of getting hurt again. What do you say?" I hold my hand out to him.

Alek stares down at my hand for what feels like an eternity before he slowly shakes it. "Deal. This fighting between us has put too much tension on Natalya. I just want her safe."

"I do, too. So, let's get her out of jail. And then let's take down Romeo and end this once and for all."

Alek's lips twitch. It's the first time he's even looked mildly pleased with me. "Let's."

Together, we walk out of my office, a tentative united front.

I'm not sure how long Alek and I will be able to work together, but when it comes to Nat, we'll burn the world down to save her.

And that's what I plan: for Nat and me to be so powerful no one will even dare question us.

Now, I just need to save my girl.

The End.

Natalya and Luca's story will finish in Sweet Union, coming out on September 12!

Grab your copy of the book NOW!

Printed in Great Britain
by Amazon

46115285R00056